My Best Friend

Kinai Gollin

Contents

Chapter one: best friends

I watch him fall onto the grass groaning as his eyes just focus above him to the sky. I roll my eyes at his childish behavior, but can't help walk over to him. I lay on the grass next to him looking up at the sky too. I watch the clouds trying to see what shape they make. A smile forms on my lips as my stomach does a flip. I hate how it always does that when I'm around him. We are best friends and now my stomach likes to flip and my heart will start to race. What's worse is people tell me I blush, but I can't tell if I do. Ugh.

"Bee, do you think I'm a fail?" He asks. My eyebrows furrow at his question making me look to him. He looks at me with a broken look on his face.

"Alex, you guys won the game." I tell him really confused.

"But I missed the goal." He points out. I roll my eyes at him. "Austin would have made the goal." He mutters.

"Dude, stop he is your brother. Plus you rocked it out there." I encourage him. He raises an eyebrow at me testing me.

"Alex!" I hear his parents call. We sit up looking at them hurrying over. My family comes too along with our other uncle. I get up quickly dusting the grass off my clothes and turn to give a hand for Alex. He takes it pulling himself up. We stand next to each other as our families come closer. Every other parent hates our parents because of how young they are. It's annoying because we get a lot of shit for it when we didn't do anything. Our parents though have told us if we ever did what they did we would be in serious trouble.

"Alex, that was a great game!" His mom cheers hugging him. He groans as she squeezes him, but hugs her back anyway. I smile at that before I'm tackled to the ground by my siblings.

"Kait, Tony get off me." I groan. I hear my parents chuckle making me send them a glare. My dad raises an eyebrow at me as my mom just glares back, playfully of course.

"You two get off your sister." My dad says. They pout, but luckily listen anyway. It's the beginning of senior year for Alex and I, which means his siblings are away as sophomores in college. It's been rough for him, and I feel bad because my siblings are younger, so I still have them. My siblings though are in eighth and sixth grade. Kait is the older one, but she acts younger than her age.

"Right, Bianca?" I blink my eyes looking to Alex's mom.

"What?" I ask completely confused. Everyone laughs making me look to them all confused.

"You guys have like all classes together this year." She says.

"Oh, yeah. Every class except art." I smile at her.

"Awe you two are too cute." She coos. Alex and I look at each other and gag, which makes everyone laugh again.

"Alright guys, lets get going. Cook out at our place." Alex's dad says. We all cheer before walking off to our cars. I can feel Alex's eyes on me, but I ignore him as I carry my brother on my back.

"Bee," Alex tries. I sigh glancing at him only to see him stop walking. I let Tony off my back, and look to Alex as Tony runs off.

"What's wrong?" I ask walking to him more. He looks to me with so much swimming in his eyes. He looks down rubbing the back of his neck before running a hair through his already messy dark brown hair.

"Nothing, lets go." He says quickly. I nod my head and we follow the rest of the group. I frown not knowing what to say to him to get him to talk.

--

I sit on the swing on the swing set just watching everyone else having fun. Alex hasn't finished getting ready yet, so I just sit here alone. Koda comes running up to me, and sits down waiting for me to pet him. I smile before reaching out scratching behind his ears. "There's that smile." I look up to see Alex walking over.

"What do you mean?" I ask feeling my smile only grow. He chuckles taking the swing beside me.

"You have been sitting here frowning for a while." He points out. I look at him raising an eyebrow.

"How would you know? You haven't been out here until now." I say looking back to Koda as I scratch him. I look to Alex hearing him talk.

"Doesn't mean I wasn't watching." He smiles, but that then turns into his nervous frown. "That sounded creepy, sorry." I laugh shaking my head.

"Alex, I know you and you are far from creepy." He smiles at me looking ahead to the rest of the 'party' here. I sigh, and Koda runs off making me frown.

"Don't fret. He just wants his mommy." He says. I nod my head, but don't look to him. "Hey, come with me. I need to show you something." He says. I can see him stand up out of the corner of my eye, but he stops in front of me. I look up to see him smiling at me as he puts his hand out for me to take. I take his hand as I stand, and he pulls me all the way to his room. Luckily no one saw us, or they would have made things weird.

"Alex, what are you doing?" I ask confused as he lets go of my hand. He shuts the door before looking at me.

"I need to tell you something. Promise me you won't say anything to anyone." I nod my head not knowing what else to do.

"Alex, are you okay?"

"I'm fine." He smiles at me. He walks towards me, and takes my hands in his. "I think I'm going to quit the soccer team." He tells me. I stare at him in utter shock. "I want to join the basketball team."

"Where is this coming from? I thought you loved soccer."

"Austin got me into it. Don't get me wrong it's a great sport, but they expect me to be just like him. I need to be me, and not just Austin's little brother." I smile at him knowing he really wants this.

"Well then, go for it." He smiles widely at me.

"Really?" He asks, excitement ringing in his voice. I smile laughing a little.

"Of course. You have to tell your family." I tell him. He takes a step back letting my hands go nodding his head understanding. I step toward and wrap my arms around him in a hug. "I'll be there if you want me to." I say reassuringly. I pull back a little to look him in the eyes. His eyes glances to my lips before looking back into my eyes. He leans in slightly as his eyes glance to my lips again. His door suddenly opens making us jump back.

"I'm sorry am I interrupting something?" Alex's dad asks. We shake our heads no as he looks us over raising an eyebrow at us.

"Dad, I need to talk to you and mom about something." Alex says. I smile at him knowing he will actually do it.

"You didn't get a girl pregnant, did you?" He asks his eyes narrowing slightly.

"What? No." Alex says. His dad raises an eyebrow at him crossing his arms over his chest.

"Then what?"

"I want mom to hear it at the same time you do, dad." Alex sighs.

"I'll just leave you two." I say walking past Alex's dad. I hurry downstairs finding my mother. I shadow her side making her look at me strangely.

"Honey, what's wrong?" She asks. I shake my head looking down. "We'll talk later." She says. I nod my head, but still stay by her. Well great, now this is awkward. We almost kissed, and I kind of wanted us to.__________
_______________________________Hoped you liked it!

If you liked please vote and comment to show me some love

Feels good to be writing with these families again

Love you all

XO

Chapter two: secrets come out

I sit on my bed finishing up some homework as my mom walks in. She takes a seat on my bed, and places a hand on my knee. "Now, Bianca what is going on?" She asks. The little party thing was two days ago, and since then I have stayed up in my room. Unless it was necessary for me to leave. That means ignoring Alex, and he has come over multiple time to try to see me.

"At the cook out, Alex and I almost kissed." I say quietly. I look into my mom's eyes waiting for her to say something, but she nods her head wanting me to keep going. "I kind of wish we did." She grins at me.

"I knew it!" She squeals. My eyebrows furrow together with confusion.

"What?"

"Sorry. Well, do you like him?" She asks a little too eagerly.

"I think so. Mom, what do I do?" She squeals again, before containing herself. "Mom, you can't tell Nicole." I tell her mind of sternly.

"Fine." She breathes out. "Why don't you just tell him how you feel?" She asks.

"Are you kidding?"

"No. I mean the poor kid thinks he did something wrong." She says. I look down nodding me head feeling bad. "Don't feel bad, honey."

"It's hard not to mom. I don't want him to hate me."

"He won't hate you." She rolls her eyes. "Oh, your father and I are going out tonight. Your siblings are sleeping over their friends' houses." I nod my head.

"Have fun." She smiles at me before standing up.

"Just talk to him hun." She smiles before leaving me alone in my room.

--

I lay on the ground in the family room just listening to the music blast through the speakers down here. I just stare up to the ceiling trying to clear my head. The music suddenly turns off making me jump up. My eyes widen as Alex leans against the door frame of the room. "Bee." He draws out. I feel my heart start to race as my eyes widen.

"Alex." I gasp. He pushes himself off the wall, and walks towards me.

"Why have you been ignoring me?" He asks. He tries to hide the hurt in his voice, but I can hear it.

"I.." I trail off not knowing what to say.

"Did I do something wrong?" He asks. His eyes show him breaking a little, and that makes my heart break. I step towards him meeting him in the middle of the room.

"It isn't you." I assure him.

"Then what's wrong, Bee? You have never ignored me before." I look down not being able to face his broken blue eyes.

"It's just..." I trail off again keeping my eyes to the ground.

"Bianca, please talk to me." Alex begs. His voice breaks me making my mouth open.

"I like you." I blurt out. Alex freezes in his spot just staring at me, and I can feel my heart beating like crazy. My stomach turns to knots as I realize the words that left my mouth. I'm surprised though as he comes towards me cupping my face before his lips are on mine. I gasp in shock from this not knowing how to respond at first, but my eyes just close as my lips move with his. He pulls away for a second, and he stays just above my lips.

"I like you too, Bianca." He whispers on my lips. I smile as his lips meet mine again, and everything goes into the kiss. I can feel me giving myself to him, and I know he is doing the same with himself.

His hands moves down my body to my hips, and they grip them tightly. I gasp in shock giving him the chance to slide his tongue in my mouth. He explores my mouth as his hands squeeze my hips. A moan escapes from me, but Alex takes it in his mouth. I pull back looking into his blue eye afraid. "Alex." I pant.

"What?" He breathes.

"I-" He cuts me off as his lips crash onto mine. I push away my fears, and wrap my arms tightly around him. I give myself to him knowing he is doing the same to me.

--

I wake up to a car door shutting. My eyes snap open landing on a naked Alex wrapped around me. My eyes widen making my heart race. Shit my parents are home! I quickly shove Alex making him fall to the ground with a thud. He pops right back up alarmed. "What's wrong?"

"My parents." I whisper shout stumbling out of bed sprinting to my closet. Alex quickly throws on his clothes and runs a hand through his hair multiple times. Once he looks fine he lounges on my bed. I throw on my pajamas and put my hair into a messy bun. Alex shakes his head at me.

"Keep your hair down." He orders. I furrow my eyebrows as we hear them enter the house. "Unless you want them to see my marks on you." He points out. I quickly fix my hair before hurrying to my desk. I turn it to be facing Alex just as my parents open my door.

"Oh, Alex. What a surprise." My mom says. I can see her winking at me making me blush. Alex chuckles nodding his head.

"Can't keep me out." He says amused.

"So, everything is good again?" My dad asks. I groan dropping my head in my hands.

"Of course, Mike." Alex chuckles. My dad groans before leaving to head to his room.

"Why don't you kids go out for a while, or better yet spend the night at Alex's." My mom says. I look at her strangely, and she gives me a wink. Then looks with her eyes after my dad.

"Oh! Yeah, um let me just change first." I say jumping up running to my closet.

"Don't do anything I wouldn't do." She chimes walking away. I throw on a pair of jeans with just a sweater. As soon as I walk out Alex pulls me down the stairs then out of the house.

"What the hell?" I pant slightly. He whips me around to face him, and his lips are on mine.

"Want me to make you pant some more?" He whispers huskily. I feel my body react as my cheeks heat up. "You seem to be walking really well." He points out.

"Adrenaline." I whisper. As the adrenaline leaves my system all the pain crashes back. "Fuck." I squeak. Alex picks me up carrying me to his house. "It's so freaking sore. I hate you."

"No you don't, now stop."__________________________________Hop ed you liked it.

So their true feeling are revealed...

Please let me know what you think but voting and commenting

Love you all

XO

Chapter three: finally together

I walk down the halls still a bit sore. Someone thinks it's funny to just take me when he wants. Okay it's not just him that wants it, but within two weeks we have done it almost every night. Today sucks more though because my monthly friend decided to show it. The meds haven't kicked in yet, I whimper as I make it to my class. I can feel Alex watching me as I take my seat. "What's wrong, Bee?" Worry clear in his voice.

"It's that time." I groan. I rest my head on my arms, that are crossed in the desk. I feel his hand start to rub my back, my lower back, to help with the pain.

"Did you have a banana this morning? I heard they are supposed to help." I groan glaring up to him.

"Shut up. I don't want to think about food. My uterus is trying to rip out of my body." I say through clenched teeth. Alex looks a little scared, but just keeps quiet as he rubs my back. The bell rings and class starts, which doesn't seem to be pleasing to my aching abdomen. I focus on my breathing, and not on the lesson the teacher has started. Alex's hand doesn't stop making me relax a little more. The pain from the cramps slowly start to disappear as the meds kick in. I let out a relived breath from the pain disappearing.

"Better?" He asks. I just nod my head giving him a small smile. He smiles back at me before he looks to the front of the room. I can't help but just watch him. I take in his strong figure, and his resemblance to his father and brother, but his blue eyes are different. They have a hint of brown in them that can tell you just how he is feeling. His eyes move to the corners to look at me, and a smirk forms on his lips. I look away bitting my lip and feeling my cheeks grow hot.

Alex groans lowly making me look to him with wide eyes. I meet his eyes and see his lust shining through them. "What?" I whisper. Alex licks his lips, and I can't help but bite mine. Just looking at his lips makes me wish they were against mine, or just my skin in general. My body heats up just thinking about what he can do. The bell rings suddenly making us both jump. Alex grabs my wrist pulling me to his chest, my back to his front.

"That damn lip bite is such a turn on." He whispers huskily in my ear. My whole body shudders from his voice.

"Alex." I groan. "Not now, or here." I whine. He huffs before letting me go. I turn to look at him, but I only see Alex putting his backpack on.

"Come on, lets get to our next class." Alex says, and I can see him change in front of me.

"Alex?"

"No, your right. Come on." He says, without looking to me. He walks pass me heading to the door, and I follow behind him.

"I'm sorry." I say before breaking down. I stop in the middle of the hall, and just let my tears fall. I look down to the ground before covering my face with my hands.

"Bee, don't cry." Alex says, as he wraps his arms around me. His arms hold me to his chest in a protective hold. I just cry into his chest, and he lets me no questions asked. "You didn't do anything wrong." He assures me. I shake my head at his words not believing him.

"Then why are you mad at me?" I cry into his chest. He sighs resting his head on mine, and I can feel him place a kiss on my head.

"I'm not mad." He assures. I look up at him with tears running down my cheeks. He cups my face wiping the tears away. "I can never be mad at you." He tells me softly. I look into his eyes seeing nothing but complete honesty.

"Then why did you just walk away?" I pout up at him. He bites his lip looking me in the eyes swallowing hard.

"I didn't want to do something I regretted." He simply states. I raise an eyebrow as the bell rings, making me jump. Alex swears under his breath, and I frown feeling guilty. "Come on." He urges, letting me go and taking my hand.

--

"Bee, are we going to tell anyone about us?" He asks. I look to him furrowing my eyebrows together.

"What do you mean?" Alex rolls his eyes at me, but a smile plays on his lips.

"About us being together." He clarifies.

"Wait, we are dating?" I gasp. Alex's eyes widen as his cheeks tint a light shade of pink.

"Um... unofficially I guess." He says. I can practically hear his heart beating out of his chest, as we sit side by side.

"Alex, we like each other. Right?" I ask. He nods his head trying to see where this is going. "Then do we have to tell people? I don't want the whole school to start rumors." He furrows his eyebrows looking into my eyes intently.

"What rumors?"

"It's happening again." I sigh. He gives me a look meaning he doesn't get one bit of it. I groan shaking my head. "Your parents." It clicks for him now as his mouth makes an 'o' shape.

"But that was years ago. No one here would bring that up. Plus they aren't us. We won't make that mistake." He states, wrapping his arms around me.

"Bee, please be my girlfriend." He begs. I smile up at him, my eyes glancing to his pouting lips.

"Okay." I grin. Alex grins too, and before I know it our lips are touching. He moves me to straddle his lap as I tilt my head to deepen the kiss. His hands grip my hips squeezing them making a moan escape my lips, which his catch. I can feel my body tingle from his touch, but I know nothing can go further right now. My hands pull at his hair making him groan into my mouth. We pull apart gasping for air, grins plastered on our lips.

"Finally, you are mine." He grins pecking my lips. I giggle at his actions, and hug him tight.

"Our parents are going to be thrilled." I laugh. I hear and feel Alex chuckle thinking about it too.

"Yeah, just wait until we tell them." He grins. He kisses my head before groaning making me pull back and look at him.

"What?"

"How much longer?" He whines, his lips pouting. I roll my eyes at him poking his nose with my finger.

"Two more days." He groans again making me laugh.

"Then I can have you, all of you?" I nod my head smiling like crazy. He smiles back, and pecks my lips before showering my face with kisses.____
_______________________________________Hope you liked it.

If you did please show it your love

Love you all

XO

Chapter four: the parents know

We walk into Alex's house hand in hand. I smile looking to our hands, knowing we are actually dating now. I'm a bit nervous to tell them, but I know nothing bad will happen. Koda runs up to us wiggling as he tries to lick us in a happy greeting. I laugh letting go of Alex's hand to pet Koda. He licks my face making me laugh.

"Koda." Alex groans. "She's mine." He whines. I look up to him grinning as I leave Koda.

"Awe, are you jealous of your dog!" I coo. Alex rolls his eyes as he wraps his arms around me. They hold me securely around my waist keeping me close to him. I can feel his body heat through his clothes, and smile at the closeness.

"Nope, because I get you all the other times." He says smugly. He sends a wink at me before kissing my lips. His lips stay there as we both melt into the kiss.

"I knew it!" We hear a squeal making us jump apart. We turn to see Alex's mom standing there clapping her hands happily. Her face holds excitement as her eyes sparkle with it.

"Mom." Alex says cautiously. She bites her lip to not squeal again as she looks between the two of us.

"I need to call Jade." She mumbles to herself. I cock my head to the side wondering why she would call my mom. "We need to start making plans." She squeals quietly. She disappears into the kitchen leaving us standing here confused.

"Plans for what?" I ask looking to Alex. He looks to me with the same look as me mirrored on his face.

"I have no freaking clue." He says. We can hear her squealing some more making us hurry into the kitchen. She stands there with her phone to her ear as she talks loudly and excitedly to, I'm guessing, my mom

"Mom?" Alex asks. She looks to us grinning.

"Jade and Mike are coming over for dinner tonight, and I think they are bringing your siblings." She says, looking to me at the last part. Alex and I look to each other groaning.

--

My parents drag my siblings in the house as my mom can't contain her excitement. She leaves my dad, and siblings, to wrap Alex and I into a tight hug. "I'm so happy for you two." She squeals loudly in my ear.

"Mom," I sigh. "We can't breathe." She quickly lets us go.

"Sorry." She smiles. Alex's mom comes into the area basically tackling my mom in a hug.

"Hey, Alex." My dad says slinging an arm around Alex's shoulders. I can see him gulp making me bite my lip to not laugh. "We are going to have a little talk later, okay?" He asks. Alex nods his head frantically, which makes my dad smile at his nervousness.

"Mike, don't scare my son so much." Alex's dad says walking into the room.

"Come on, lets sneak away until dinner." Alex whispers in my ear. I nod my head, and he pulls me outside to his back yard. The wind blows making a chill run through my body, but I ignore it. We breath in the free air sighing in content.

"Well, I think it's going better than expected." He laughs. I smile at him as he takes my hand.

"I'm still worried about what the school will think." I whisper looking back out to the swing set. Alex stops walking, and turns me to look at him.

"Don't worry about it. Just ignore them. I want to be with you, and you want to be with me. No mater what people say it won't change that." He tells me. I can hear the truth in his words, and his eyes lock with mine.

"W-" Alex cuts me off with his lips claiming mine. I melt into the kiss leaning in more. We both ignore the possibilities of our parents watching us from inside, because in this moment it is only us.

His arms wrap around my waist pulling me closer to him. Our bodies keeping each other warm from the slight chilliness in the air. Our lips move in sync with each other's, and I tilt my head to the side so we can deepen the kiss. The feeling of his lips on mine creates chaos in my stomach, and my heart tries to come out of my chest.

"Hey! Get your lips off my daughter!" We jump apart turning to look at my dad. My eyes go wide, and my heart races even more watching him glare at Alex.

"I'm sorry, Mike." Alex sighs. My dad just narrows his eyes on him.

"Act like I'm always watching, boy, because I am." He says before shutting the door. I look to Alex fear written clearly across my face. He seems calm though.

"Don't freak out, Bee. Your dad loves me." He grins. He pecks my lips before pulling me in for a hug. "Come on, lets go inside and face them." He sighs, picking me up. I squeal in surprise making him chuckle. We walks us back into the house before letting me down.

"That was gross." Tony, my brother, gags. I only smile at him before ruffling his hair.

"Not my fault you were watching." I say in a sing song voice. He rolls his eyes before walking away.

"Honey, it's time for dinner." My mom says. I smile walking towards the dinning room. I feel Alex right behind me, and my stomach starts to go crazy from the nerves. I feel his hand slip into mine giving it an encouraging squeeze. I lean into his touch as I look where to sit. Luckily there are two spots left right next to each other. We take a seat, and Alex rests a hand comfortably on my thigh. I watch my dad narrow his eyes on him.

"Boy, hands where I can see them." He says. Alex stiffens before placing his hands on the table.

"Mike." My mom scolds. He looks to her raising an eyebrow.

"Yes?"

"Leave the poor boy alone." She says.

"But, we all know what happens when they can't keep their hands to themselves." He points out.

"That hurt, dude." Alex's dad says. Mike just shrugs looking to him.

"Wow, Mike." Alex's mom says. "And here I thought you were our friend."

"Hey, we did the same thing. Just a few years after you two." He argues. Then they all start laughing as Alex and I look to each other in disgust.

"He isn't wrong though." He whispers in my ear. He does it so only I can hear, and at his words my body stiffens a little. "I love it when you blush." He grins. I feel my eyes widen because I can't even tell that I am.

"So, how long?" Nicole, Alex's mom, asks eagerly. We look to her, then to each other before back to her.

"Like a day."

"Really?" My mom awes. I nod my head smiling to her.

"Seems longer." Nicole says.

"Mom, we've known each other for like ever. We just slid right into it."

"Not literally though, right?" My dad asks. My eyes widen, and Alex chokes on his water.

"N-No sir." He stutters. I shoot him a glare for stuttering.

"Ummm... sure." My dad says. He eyes Alex like a hawk watching his ever move, and taking in every detail.

"Just use protection, that's all we ask." Justin, Alex's dad, says.

"Justin! I don't want to know what he is doing to my daughter." My dad groans.

"I didn't tell you to think about it."

"Boys." My mom and Nicole say at the same time. This is going to be a long night.__________________________________Hope you liked it.

If you did please show this story some love

Love you all

XO

Chapter five: spreading

W e walk down the halls at school holding hands. We can see people give us looks, but we ignore it. I sigh as we reach my locker, which we share. Our friends Chris and Nini are waiting there watching us with big grins. "Congrats you two!" Nini cheers hugging us. She lets go, and takes a step back. I smile at her as I move to do the combination to open my locker. After getting it open Alex and I put our jackets in there. It's sadly starting to get cold out, and I don't like the cold.

"Way to go man, finally got the balls." Chris grins clapping Alex on the back. "Oh, and coach wanted to see you. The scouts are starting to talk to him, and will be coming this spring." He adds. I can see Alex tense a little making me frown. I wrap my arms around his waist, and kiss his chest. He relaxes as he looks down to me, and his arms wrap around me.

"I'll talk to him." He states. Chris just nods his head. "Ugh, I got to get to class. Forgot to do the homework." Chris groans. We nod at him, and he drags himself away.

"You guys are so cute." Nini awes. I smile nuzzling my head into his chest. I hear some whispers before the loud sound of a picture on a phone being taken. I look up to see someone freeze standing in front of us. She quickly hurries off, and I look to Alex worried.

"Everything will be fine, Bee." He assures me. He leans down kissing my lips quick.

"Damn, you guys are fucking goals." Nini states in awe. I look to her smiling shyly. "If that bitch starts anything I got her." She tells me. I laugh at that as Alex lets me go. I close my locker, and we start to just walk around the halls.

--

I walk into art, and everyone watches me. Smirks plastered on their faces, and a look of amusement masking them. "Look who is going down the same path." One girl sneers pointing at me. Everyone laughs making me keep my head down.

"Oh, what's wrong? Family disowned you?" Some guy laughs. I take my seat, but gasp as I look to the table. There is a picture taped on it, the one of Alex and I from this morning. There is a red arrow pointing to my stomach with writing.

Looks like there is a bun in the oven guys, they wanted to be just like their parents. How touching.

I feel tears prick my eyes as I look up to all the laughing faces. "I'm not fucking pregnant!" I yell at them. They stop laughing, and study me.

"You sure about that?" Some girl asks eyeing me up and down.

"Are you calling me fat?" I ask raising an eyebrow as I stand up. She stands up too crossing her arms over her chest. Her blond hair is long flowing over her back in curls. Her blue eyes narrow on me in an intimidating way, but it doesn't phase me. Her face has makeup caked on making her look like an orange.

"I was calling you a knocked up whore, but in that case... yes. You are a fat little, slut." She says. Without me realizing it my hand comes up slapping her across the face. Everyone gasps, but I don't care. I not going to be bullied for dating Alex.

Next think I know she has me on the floor trying to hurt me. I push her off me pinning her down to the ground. I throw a punch at her eye, before a second one to her nose. She screams in pain, and people grab me trying to pull me off.

"That's enough!" I hear our teacher shout. Two guys in the class hold me back. I look to see her on the ground, and spit on her. "Escort her to the office." He orders. The two guys do it with no questions asked.

"You can let me go, you know?" I tell them. They give me a look before nodding their heads and letting me go. I sigh in relief as I continue to walk to the office. They walk next to me, and I can feel them sneaking glances at me the whole time. I stop walking, and so do they, which I turn to look at them.

"Do you believe her along with the rest of them?" I ask, looking to each of them. They look to each other then back to me not knowing what to say. "Ugh you do." I groan. "I can see it in your eyes."

"Bianca," One sighs, his name is AJ. "I don't believe them. Everyone is different, and you aren't your parents." He assures. I smile at him as he runs a hand through his hair.

"Thank you AJ." I smile.

"So, you and Alex?" The other one, Jack, asks. I can't help the blush as I nod my head.

"We, should probably start walking again. Don't worry we will tell Mr. Weber what actually happened." AJ says. I smile at him nodding my head.

"Thank you." I say ask we start walking.

--

I walk to my locker sighing happy the day is done. Mr. Weber left me with a warning after the guys explained what went down. My cheek hurts like hell from the way she slapped, and scratched it. I open my locker, and reach for my books. "Bee?" I hear his voice. I look to him a smile forming on my lips.

"Hey." I smile going to kiss his cheek. He stops me holding me in front of him. He right hand comes up cupping my cheek gently. He rubs his thumb on it making me flinch.

"Who did this to you?" He asks, his eyebrows furrowing together.

"Some girl in my art class." I sigh. He pulls me in for a hug, his arms wrapping around my waist. I melt in his touch resting my cheek carefully on his chest.

"I'm sorry." He whispers. "I'm sorry you had to deal with that."

"It's fine, Alex. Has anyone said anything to you?" I can feel him go tense making me force myself to look up at him.

"Some people said some choice words." He says not looking into my eyes. I hold his face in my hands.

"Alex, look at me." I tell him. His blue eyes lock with mine, and I can see his uncertainty. "You don't want to do this, do you?" I force out through the lump in my throat.

"What? No. Bee, I just don't want you to go through all that shit."

"Alex, its already spreading through the school. There will be people on both sides, and we will just have to push through it." I say. His lips twitch into a smile.

"This is why I chose you." He says, his lips turning into a grin. I grin back kissing his lips.

"Aye, love birds." Chris calls. We jump apart to see Chris and Nini walking up to us. We smile at them, with my cheeks heating up, and Alex's turning slightly pink.

"Girl, we got to get going to the library." I groan nodding my head. I look to Alex, who is watching me with his sparkling eyes.

"I got practice, so I'll see you after." I nod my head.

"Which one?" I ask quietly.

"Basketball doesn't start until next month. So, I'm still working out with the soccer team for now. Don't worry Bee, I'll be playing both sports." He says pulling me closer to him.

"Wait, dude you are playing basketball too?" Chris asks. I can feel Alex tense with his arms around me, and I sigh knowing he hasn't told him yet.

"Yeah." He sighs.

"That's great! I was thinking about hopping it this year too! I was told I got skill, but didn't want to join alone." I feel Alex relax, and he lets me go to look at Chris.

"Really?"

"Hell yeah! Yo lets go talk to coach." He says, excitement running through both of them. Nini and I laugh watching them. Alex turns to me kisses my cheek, and they take off running. I look to Nini sobering up from laughing.

"This should be fun."

"Oh yeah." She agrees. "Come on, lets go."________________________

_________Hope you liked it

If you did please show it some love.

Love you all

XO

Chapter six: secrets

Nini lays on my bed next to me finally done with homework. I finish my last paper, and push my stuff of my bed not caring. I glance over to her and see her biting her lip. I roll to my side and look to her. "What's up?" I ask. She looks to me her brown eyes clouded over.

"What do you mean?" She asks innocently. I roll my eyes at her.

"You know what I mean. Just tell me what's up?" I ask. She lets out a long breath before looking into my eyes.

"I like him." She says. My eyebrows furrow not knowing who she is talking about. I gasp feeling my eyes widening.

"Alex?"

"No! Not Alex." She assures looking at me afraid. I raise an eyebrow at her waiting. "Chris."

"Really?" I squeal. I practically jump on her excitedly, and her eyes widen.

"Yes."

"That's great!"

"Bianca, he doesn't like me back. How do I even go about it?"

"Nini, you don't know that. You just have to talk to him, you know? Find out what he feels." She gives me the 'are you kidding' look, and I roll my eyes.

"I can't do that." She states. I can hear the nervousness in her voice, which makes me sigh at her.

"Can't or won't?" I test raising an eyebrow at her. She bites her lip sitting up looking away. "Nini?"

"I'm scared, Bianca. What if he doesn't feel the same way?" I sit up, and rest a hand comfortably on her shoulder.

"Don't freak out. What me to do some detective work first?" I ask. She looks to me hopeful, which makes a smile form on my lips.

"Can you?"

"Of course I can." I grin.

"Just don't tell Alex. I know you tell him everything, but please don't." I nod my head smiling.

"I promise."

--

I curl into Alex's side sighing in content. We are currently cuddling on his couch in the family room. His parents are home, and want to make sure we aren't doing anything bad. Alex groaned annoyed, but I just laughed pulling him. Now, his arms are around me protectively making me feel safe.

"How was practice?" I ask tracing small shapes on his arm. His arms tighten around me as his lips kiss my head.

"It was great. Coach is unsure about the whole thing with Chris and I joining the basketball team." I look up to him, and he spaces out staring at nothing in front of him. I stretch up to place a kiss on his cheek. He blinks before looking to me grinning. His lips find mind, and I sigh smiling into the kiss.

"I want you so bad." He words whisper on my lips. I can feel my body heat up from his words as my arms wrap around him.

"We can't."

"Not here." He says pulling back. He looks around, and finds his mom in the kitchen. "Hey, mom?" She looks up smiling.

"What?"

"We are going to head out, I want to take Bee out for dinner." She grins at us nodding her head.

"Be careful you two." She says. We get up from the couch and walk to the door to slip on our shoes. "Don't stay out too late."

"Mom its Friday." Alex pouts. She raises an eyebrow at him.

"Does it look like I care?"

"Fine." He lets out. We hurry out the door, and to his car. Once we are in I look to him, and he starts the car.

"Where are we going?"

"I know a place." Alex looks to me smirking. I groan buckling up as he starts to drive.

--

I look at the little apartment in confusion. It is fully furnished with pictures Alex seemed to put around. "When the hell did you get this place?" I look to him as he shuts the door.

"Oh, I got it a few months back. My parents don't know about it because I pay for it myself."

"How?" I feel my eyes widen. He shifts on his feet looking to the ground.

"I have a job at this business. They wanted to try working with seniors in high school, and hired me." My eyebrows furrow as I take it in.

"But you never said anything about going to work."

"It was for a magazine, and a commercial. They wanted to get their clothing line out there." He says.

"How come I haven't seen it anywhere?"

"It's in Australia, and you can't tell anyone about it." He walks up to me smiling shyly. "Now, can we finish what we started at my house?" I grin wrapping my arms around his neck.

"I think so." He grins leaning in. His lips claim mine, and I can't help the moan that escapes from how good his lips feel.

--

I snuggle into his side wanting to be closer to his warm body. His arms are possessively around my waist as he sleeps. My eyes open, and I blink into the dark room. I glance to the clock on his night stand, which making my eyes widen. Alex's mom is going to be furious. I look up to see him still sleeping. I roll my eyes before I move and shove him off the bed. He groans as he lands with a thud.

"What the hell?"

"It's two in the morning!" I panic. His eyes snap open wide to me. He jumps up, and starts looking to get his clothes on.

"Where are our clothes?" He panics looking around.

"I think in the living area." We rush out there to see our clothes. We quickly throw them on, and make ourselves look presentable. Then we leave in a rush trying to make it home quickly.

"You are coming with me. My mom might get suspicious if you don't." Alex sounds out of breath, and I know we are both worn out.

"Okay. I'm sorry she is going to be pissed." I whisper, looking down to my lap.

"Bee, it isn't your fault. Don't think that. That was fucking amazing." He tells me truthfully. I feel my cheeks heat up still not looking up.

"Will they know?" I ask my eyes snapping wide. They will probably be able to freaking smell it on us. I can feel my heart start to race knowing they will find out. And hand on my thigh makes me jump slightly, but with his thumb rubbing soothing circles I calm down.

"Don't worry, Bee. They won't know." He assures me. We pull into his driveway, and quietly make our way into his house. Koda barks before he sees us, and I can feel my body tense. Alex wraps an arm around my shoulders as he leads us in. As soon as we shut the door lights turn on.

"What did I tell you?" Alex's mom asks. Her hands are on her hips, and her head is tilted to the side. She looks pissed, but behind her Alex's dad looks beyond pissed. He is fuming with his arms crossed over his chest.

"Where the hell were you?" He demands. I can feel Alex tense against me, making me freak out more. Alex glances to me, and I look to him. Our eyes meet, which calms me down a little._______________________________

_____Hope you liked it

If you did please give it some love

Love you all

XO

Chapter 7: grounded

I sit on my bed doing homework yawning. After Alex and I got in trouble for coming home late we have been grounded. If he is over he has to leave by six, and if I'm over his it's the same deal. It's been a rough month if you ask me. Nini is over right now helping me finish some assignment I didn't understand. I feel her looking at me groaning.

"What's up?" I ask her. She looks to me holding her stomach.

"Period cramps. Do you have to meds?" She asks. I nod my head getting off the bed. I head over to my bathroom, and grab a bottle of meds. I bring them back to her, but as I walk back in my room I freeze. I nearly drop the meds, but grip them tighter.

"Bianca?" Nini questions, forcing herself up. I blink shaking my head. I walk to her handing her the bottle. "Thank you. Are your okay, though?" She takes the bottle opening it. She takes what she needs and downs the dry.

"Yeah, I'm fine. It's just this being grounded thing is annoying." She nods her head as she closes the pills.

"Tell me about it. With both of you being grounded it's only Chris and I, but he doesn't want to do anything." I shake my head smiling at her annoyance.

"At least you can go have fun if you want to."

"Bianca, you time is up! Sorry Nini." My mom calls up. I frown looking to Nini, who only sighs getting up. She hugs me tight before walking out of my room. I let out a breath as I fall down on my bed. How late am I? I count the days constantly in my head. My heart races a little more each time. I close my eyes feeling tears want to fall out. I hear my siblings run into my room making me jump up.

"What's up?" I ask forcing a smile. They both study me before shrugging.

"Mom said you will help up with our homework." I nod my head.

"Go get your work." They grin before running off. They might be in different grades, but they still don't want to do their homework. Definitely not by themselves. They run back in climbing on my bed, and looking up to me.

"Please help me first." Tony begs. I laugh nodding my head.

"Okay, Kait start yours and I'll help you after." She nods her head, and focuses on her homework. I look to see Tony needs help with math, which makes me groan.

"What's wrong?" Tony asks looking up to me with innocent eyes.

"It's math. I don't do good with math, but I'll try." He smiles at me looking back down.

--

My eyes snap open before I fling myself off my bed racing for the bathroom. Emptying my stomach of whatever could still be in there into the toilet. I groan wiping my mouth with toilet paper, and throwing that in the toilet. Flushing it I stand up, and walk to the sink. Rinsing my mouth out before I splash my face with cold water. I look in the mirror to see I'm not pale, so I can't be sick. My eyes widen as I count the days over and over again.

"Shit, I'm late." I walk back to my bed sinking down into it. "It has to be stress." I tell myself. I look to the clock, and see it's time to get ready for school. I force myself to head to my closet, and look for an outfit. I pick out light jeans, which I cuff at the ankle, and a blue flowy short sleeve top. I top it off with a long necklace, and slip my white converse on. I put the clothes on before hurrying to the bathroom again, throwing up. I stand up again rinsing my mouth, and then brushing my teeth.

"Bianca, hurry or you will be late!" I hear my mom call. I gulp finishing up before walking to the stairs. My stomach feels weird, and my nerves go on overdrive as I take slow steps down the stairs. I take a gulp as I walk into the kitchen, and there my mom is making breakfast.

"I got to go, Alex is picking me up." I get out. She looks to me, and her eyes study me. She raises an eyebrow putting her hands on her hips.

"What's up with you?" She asks.

"W-What?" I stutter.

"You are being jumpy, and nervous as hell." She points out. "Honey, have some breakfast first." I look to the food, and feel my stomach churn. I shake my head looking back to her.

"Nope I'm good, I have to get going though." I grab my backpack and sling it around my shoulder.

"Are you sure? You never miss breakfast. Are you feeling okay?" She bombards me with questions.

"Mom, I'm fine. I really got to go though." She just nods her head watching me, and I swear I can hear her gasp. I ignore it as I open the door and walk out. I start heading over towards Alex's, and stop seeing him leave his house. He looks up his eyes meet mine. A grin forms on his lips, and I can't help the smile that forms on mine. He jogs over to me wrapping his arms around me.

"I missed you." Alex showers my face with kisses making me giggle. "We are finally free from our cruel punishment." He cheers. I roll my eyes before placing a quick kiss on his lips.

"Come on, lets get to school." I say. What if I get sick in his car? He would kill me, but that's a risk I have to take.

"Okay." He opens the passenger door for me smiling. "Ladies first." I feel my cheeks heat up as I smile. I get in the car, and he shuts the door. I watch him jog around to the driver's side, and get in. I put my seatbelt on as he does his. He starts the car, and I rest my head on the head rest. His places his hand on my thigh, which only makes me sigh in content.

Maybe I'm just overthinking things, and maybe I am sick. I should have stayed home today. I feel the car stop, and hear Alex shut it off. I open my eyes to see we are at school. "Bee, are you okay?" I hear his gently concerned voice ask. I look to him putting on the best smile I can.

"Yeah, I'm fine. We should probably start heading in." I sigh. He nods his head, and we get out. I put my backpack on, and we start walking to the school. Once inside I feel my stomach churn again. My eyes widen, and I hurry to the nearest trash bin. I feel someone hold my hair back, and rub small circles around my back. Once done I pull away and walk towards the nearest bathroom.

"Bee, you should be home. You're sick." Alex says. He follows me in the bathroom, which luckily is empty. He shuts the door, and locks it so no one else can come in.

"Alex, I'm fine." I say wiping my mouth. I rinse it out again, and sigh looking to him. His eyes study me trying to read me. See what is wrong with me.

"Are you hungover?" I roll my eyes at him.

"I don't drink idiot." I cross my arms over my chest.

"Are you stressed?" I can see him grow nervous by the second. I nod my head shrugging off the last option we don't want to say. He lets out a sigh in relief. "Why are you so stressed?"

"School, college stuff. Ugh there is so much I have to do. Not to mention the other work teachers throw at us." Alex wraps his arms around me holding me close.

"One step at a time, Bee. Don't stress, you are way ahead of most people. You don't have to worry." He soothes. I nod my head nuzzling it in his chest. The door unlocks, and some guy comes in, wearing janitor clothes.

"What is going on in here?"

"She was having a panic attack, and I had to help her." Alex easily lies. The guy nods his head studying us.

"Okay, now get out. This is the ladies room." Alex nods his head, before leading me out. I clutch to his side, and he keeps me close to his side.

I just hope this is all just stress.____
Hope you liked it.

If you did please show it some love

Love you all

XO

Chapter 8: guess it runs in the family

I rush up to my room hiding the bag, and hurry into my attached bathroom. Locking the door I do what needs to be done. I still throw up every morning, and it's been a week. I finally forced myself to take the step to figure this out. Placing it on the counter I slide down the wall until my butt hits the floor. I wrap my arms around my knees as I wait. Tears start stinging my eyes wanting to fall. I hear the timer go off, but I can't move as tears start to spill.

I sit on the tile floor not wanting to look and see. He has no clue, and I don't think I could tell him. I don't even think I would be able to face my parents. I look up through my leaking eyes, and see it on the counter. I can't bring myself to stand, and look at it.

This wasn't supposed to happen to me, to us. We were so careful about it all, and now I'm here crying, and praying. Even though I know what is happening.

There is only one thought running through my head, my best friend's what?

I force myself up and stand there shaking, and my eyes land on the positive sign. I cup my hands over my mouth as tears blur my vision. This can't be happening, I'm having my best friend's baby. Suddenly the bathroom door opens, and I hear a gasp. I look to see my mom standing there taking in the scene. Instead of screaming she opens her arms up for me tears in her eyes. I run into her arms, and sob into her shirt.

"It's okay, honey. We will get through this." She assures me. I shake my head knowing nothing can make this okay. She hugs me tighter telling me over and over everything will be alright. "You have to tell him."I pull away looking up at her.

"I can't do that, mom. He will hate me. I ruined his college future." I try wiping my tears as I talk. I feel her hug me tighter as she rubs my back soothingly.

"He won't hate you. You have to tell him though. Don't do what Nicole did, she waited and Justin figured it out on his own. He didn't really take it well at first." I look up to her confusion clouding my mind.

"Alex's parents?" She nods her head. "Mom, I'm scared." She gives me a frown as a tear slides down her cheek.

"I know honey, but it will be fine." She lets me go, and walks towards the counter looking to the test. "I knew from that first day you wouldn't eat, but I was waiting to be sure." I hear her.

"I'm sorry mom. I didn't mean for it to happen." She looks up to me with a small smile.

"No one ever means for this to happen at your age." She tells me.

"Dad's going to kill him." My eyes wide. She chuckles at me, which makes me look to her like she is crazy.

"Unless Justin kills him first."

"Oh god." I gasp putting an hand over my heart. "When do I tell him?"

"Now."

"But he ask basketball practice." I look to the tile floor trying to take deep breathes. "How do I do it?"

"You just hold his hand and look him in the eyes, and say Alex I'm pregnant." She says. My siblings fall into the bathroom eyes wide.

"You're pregnant!" They shout looking at me with wide eyes. I look to them with wide eyes glancing to our mom for help.

"You breathe a word of this to your father and you two will be in big trouble." Mom warns. "She will tell him later tonight." I look to her ready to break.

"Please." I beg them.

"Okay, but Bianca I'm going to kick Alex in the balls." Tony says. I roll my eyes at him.

"Tony, we should cut them off." Kait proposes. He grins before they run off.

"Poor Alex."

--

I take deep breathes trying to calm my frantic beating heart. Alex walks up to me with his usual grin on, but it soon disappears taking me in. "Bee, what's wrong?" I hesitantly stand up, and take his hand.

"You should sit down." I tell him. I watch the fear in his eyes as he looks at me.

"You better not be breaking up with me." He can only whisper.

"What? Gosh no. I could never do that. I have to tell you something." He takes a seat slowly looking into my eyes. I take a deep breath ready to talk. "Remember earlier this week when I was throwing up?" I nods his head stiffly.

"Yeah, you were stressed about college." He says. I shake my head feeling my stomach flip.

"I've been doing that all week so far. Alex I-"

"Please don't say it." He begs. I look at him feeling me eyes sting with tears. My vision becomes blurry as I take in a hurt breath.

"I'm pregnant." I tell him. He lets my hand go as he rubs his hands up and down his face. He looks away from me standing up. He starts pacing the floor in my room. I stand there unsure what to do.

"How do you know?" I sigh walking into the bathroom. I grab the test and bring it out to him. Alex takes it in his hands studying it. "You should go to the doctor to make sure." He snaps looking up to me.

"I have an appointment."

"Who is the father?" I step back as if he hit me. His eyes show anger. "Bianca, we haven't had sex for a good month if not more. Not since we got grounded."

"That's how long it takes to see the signs sometimes a little longer." I tell him hurt coating my words. He looks stunned as he looks down at the test then to me.

"Its mine?" I nod my head. "We are having a baby?" I nod my head, a small smile playing on my lips.

"Yes." Alex wraps me in a protective hug. Tears fall freely from my eyes, and Alex cups my face making me look up to him.

"We are having a baby." He grins kissing my lips.

"You're what!" We jump to see my dad in the doorway.

"Mike, just let them have their moment." My mom groans from outside the doorway. My dad glares at Alex, and I feel Alex stiffen behind me.

"Is this true?"

"Is what true?"

"Did you, or did you not knock up my daughter?" Alex and I look at each other gulping.

"Yes." Alex says, looking back to my dad. My dad steps forward jaw clench and hands in fists.

"How could you be so careless?" He asks. I take a step back feeling stabbed by my own father.

"Mike!" My mom shouts coming into the room. She looks to us smiling. "One moment." She then glares at my father, and grabs his ear dragging him out. I look to Alex with my eyes blurring, and his take me in widening. His arms are around me instantly bringing me to him.

"Shh it's okay. Everything will be okay." He assures me. I shake my head though knowing it won't be like we hope.

"No it's not." He looks hurt by my words, but tries to cover it.

"B-"

"Alex, your parents are going to be worse. The school will tare us apart because of this. Our poor baby." I cry. I feel his lips press a lingering kiss on my forehead.

"Don't worry about that now, everything will okay. I promise we will get through this."____Hope you liked it

If you did like it please show it some love

Love you all

XO

Chapter 9: this can't be real

I hold Alex's hand tightly as we walk through school. After school we have an appointment to confirm the pregnancy, which scares me to death. I keep my head down not wanting to catch glances from any of the other students in here. I feel bad because Alex is missing basketball practice to come with me, but he told me not to worry. It took everything in me to get up this morning, and I just wanted to curl up after throwing up. We reach my locker, and I look up to see Nini and Chris waiting for us. I look to Alex with wide eyes, and he just gives me small slime as he squeezes my hand reassuringly.

"Hey, good morning." Chris grins. I smile back, which me swallowing my nerves down. Nini comes up and hugs me tightly. Chris and Alex do some handshake before I feel both of Alex's arms around me. Nini steps back closer to Chris, which I raise an eyebrow to. She blushes looking away from me, and I make a note to ask her about it later.

"So, practice is supposed to be pretty chill today." Chris tells Alex.

"I'm not going to practice today, I got to let coach know soon." Chris frowns at him.

"Why not man?" Alex rolls his eyes glancing to me quick. He knows not to say anything until we figure this out for sure.

"Dude, I got a doctor's appointment. My mom is forcing me to go, but I zoned her out as she was babbling on." Chris shakes his head a smile on his face.

"That's got to suck bro." Alex shrugs his shoulders. I lean more into his chest needing to feel more comfort.

"Bianca, we are still on for the library right?" Nini asks smiling. I frown forgetting she wanted to do a project there.

"I'm sorry, my mom is forcing me to go shopping with the kids. She wants my input on options." I groan annoyed. Nini frowns at me, but nods her head sighing.

"Tomorrow?"

"Of course, I'm sorry."

"Don't be."

"Girls, we should head off to our classes." Alex tells us. I frown as I look to him, and pout. He tries to stay strong not wanting to give in. "Bee, we have to." He sighs kissing my lips. I smile against his lips making him smile.

"I'm sorry, are we not here." Chris calls. Alex pulls away, and I roll my eyes before glaring at Chris. "Come on guys, lets get to class." He tries to sound enthusiastic, but that's far from how he said it.

--

I sit nervously holding tightly onto Alex's hand, and my mom has a hand on my knee. The door opens the doctor walking in a bright smile on her face. She seems tired, but forces happiness out for us to absorb. "Congratulations." She smiles shutting the door. I feel my heart stop for a second as my eyes widen. "You are pregnant. It is a little too early to do an ultrasound, so we will have to schedule one."

"Really?" I ask unsure. She nods her head showing me the results of the test. I feel Alex squeeze my hand making me look to him.

"It's going to be okay." He assures me. I feel a tear run down my cheek, and he wipes it away.

"I'll just go set up the appointment." I hear my mom before her and the doctor leave. Alex wraps his arms around me, and I just cry in his arms. He rubs my back trying to comfort me, but it just makes me cry more. Everyone is going to say shit about us, and I know school is going to be hell now. They were all right, we are just like them.

"Your parents are going to kill us." I hiccup out resting my head on his shoulder. Alex lets out a big sigh his arms tightening around me.

"They will be pissed, but don't worry about it." He says. I shake my head pulling away from him.

"They will hate me, disown you. I can't believe I did this to you." Alex gently grabs my face in his hands making me look in his eyes.

"They will not do that to me. Bee, it takes two to make a baby. Don't blame yourself for our baby." His lips meet mine, and I can't help melting into him. My eyes flutter close, and I feel all the problems leave. We pull apart needing air, and Alex rests his forehead on mine.

"We should get going." I whisper.

"Okay." He pulls back helping me off the table, which makes me roll my eyes. We head out of the room, and walk back to the waiting room area.

We spot my mom at the desk with the doctor. She looks up to us sighing, and tells the doctor something before walking to us.

"You two ready?" She asks. I nod my head squeezing Alex's hand. "Okay good. Now, we have to tell your parents." She says looking to Alex.

"Ready as I'll ever be." He sighs. My mom gives him a small smile before looking to me.

"I want you two to know I am here to support you guys. I may not be thrilled, but I will be there when ever you need me. I will even be there when you tell Nicole, and Justin." I smile at my mom as her eyes meet mine.

"Thank you." She hugs me smiling.

"You don't have to thank me for being your mother." She laughs a little.

"Thank you." Alex says, as she pulls away from me.

"You don't have to thank me either. Your baby is my grandchild after all. How could I hate it?" He cracks a smile at that. "We should probably head back. I got to get home for Kait and Tony." My mom sighs. We head out to the car, and the first thought that runs through my head is I'm having my best friend's baby. I don't know what this means for us, but I hope nothing bad. Alex takes my hand in his squeezing it. I look up to him smiling.

"What's running through your mind?" He asks raising an eyebrow.

"Just that I'm having a baby with my best friend." He smiles at me letting my hand go only to wrap his arm around my shoulder.___________
____________________Hope you liked it, sorry it's a little short. So it's official...

If you did like it please show it some love

Love you all

XO

Chapter 10: breaking the news

I hesitantly sit back in my seat as I feel eyes on me. Alex had a hand on my right knee rubbing soothing circles with his thumb. I try to let it soothe me, but the thought of Alex's parents hating us freaks me out. "Bianca, honey are you okay?" I hear Nicole, his mom, ask. I look up to her my eyes widening.

"Y-yeah." I stutter. I feel my mom kick me under the table making me look to her. She gives me a pointed look, and I take a deep breath. "Nicole, I'm pregnant." I tell her as my eyes meet hers. I watch her eyes widen as her face pales slightly. I feel Justin glare at Alex as he stiffens beside me.

"I'm sorry, did I hear that right?" She asks. I gulp nodding my head. "Alex, is it yours?" She asks.

"Mom! Bianca could never do that to me. Yes it's mine." He says appalled she would think that. I feel tears prick my eyes as I think of how much she hates me now. Along with Alex because we both got into this situation. It also hurts that she thought I could cheat on Alex.

"I thought we taught you better than that." I hear Justin, Alex's dad, scolds.

"I know dad. It's not like we planned this, but it happened." Alex's voice sounds ashamed. I feel like he stabs me with his words, and it kills. I quickly stand up ignoring the calls as I head outside. I just can't be around them right now. Tears fall from my eyes, and I sit on the front stoop. I hold my knees to my chest resting my head on my knees.

"Bianca?" My head snaps up seeing Austin walking up the driveway. He has a backpack on, and a duffle bag in his right hand. He looks concerned watching me cry. He quickly walks up to me, and drops his bags before wrapping me in a hug. "What's wrong?" I shake my head no not wanting to get anymore hate, that I can't handle. "You can tell me." He assures. I look him in the eyes taking a deep breath.

"Austin, I'm pregnant." I whisper. His eyes widen taken back from my answer.

"Really? Who do I have to beat up? I swear this kid is going to have to help support." He starts going off, just as I hear the front door open.

"B- wait Austin?" Alex questions not expecting his brother.

"Hey bro. Wait, did you get pissed at her?" He questions Alex in a hard voice.

"What? No. Bianca whatever I said I'm sorry."

"It's how you said it." I choke out leaving Austin's arms standing up, and Austin stands up too. "You don't want it do you." I state.

"Bee, don't think like that. Of course I want this, it's just going to be hard."

"Hold up. What is going on?" Austin says totally confused. Alex and I look to each other before we look to Austin. "Wait, you got her pregnant?"

"Yeah."

"Way to go, finally grew a pair and asked her out. I'm proud bro, but maybe the baby was a bit much." Austin seems to be taking this lightly. Alex rolls his eyes at his brother. "How did mom and dad take it?"

"That's what we are doing now."

"Oh, let me go lighten the mood." He smiles grabbing his bags, and striding into the house. Alex looks to me his eyes guilty, which makes me frown.

"Bee, I really am fine with this. I'm not mad or ashamed." He assures me. I walk towards him, and he opens his arms up for me. I walk into his embrace, and his arms wrap around me keeping me safe. I breath in his scent calming myself down.

"Sorry, emotions are high." I whisper. Alex chuckles kissing my head.

"We should head inside." I sigh at his words looking up to him.

"Okay, but how mad are they?" He shakes his head at me.

"Find out for yourself." He says. I pout wanting to know what he means. Alex just chuckles kissing my pouting lips before letting me go. He takes my hand leading me into the house. We hear laughter coming from the kitchen making my eyebrows furrow.

"And then he fell into the lake. It was hilarious." Austin gets out in between laughs. We walk into the room, and everyone looks to us trying to stop their laughter. Must have been some funny story. "Hey, you two." Austin grins sobering up.

"Oh Austin." I sigh shaking me head. He only grins wider at that. Alex's parents and my mom grow quiet just staring at Alex and I.

"All right, now lets address the elephant in the room. Alex I'm sorry bro, but you need to leave." Austin says in all seriousness.

"What?"

"Like leave, your fat self is taking up all of Bianca's oxygen, and space." I glance to Alex cracking a smirk, but he just rolls his eyes.

"Austin, be nice to your brother." Nicole scolds.

"Mom, I'm not five. Plus it's my job." Austin states. She raises an eyebrow at him crossing her arms over her chest. "Sorry mommy, I love you." He squeaks out. I try not to laugh watching him.

"Now, Alex." Justin says turning everyone's attention on Alex. "We are not thrilled, but we are here for you. I'm pretty sure we will be excited for you two in a few weeks, but it has to sink in." He glances to Nicole.

"My first grandchild!" She tries not to squeal. "I didn't think it would happen this soon, but I guess one of you had to follow our footsteps." Nicole starts mumbling.

"Wait, your not mad? You don't hate us?" I question still so unsure. They chuckle looking to each other before looking back to us.

"Of course not, honey. We could never be mad for something we did, even if we don't approve." Nicole says getting up from her seat. She walks over to us, and wraps us in a tight hug. I hug her back feeling the tears sting my eyes, again, but this time for a different reason.

"Mom, your hurting us." Alex groans.

"Shh I'm not. Stop being a boy." She scolds quietly. I hold in a laugh as he grunts in response.

"How come I never get that kind of hug?" Austin pouts.

"Austin, not everything is about you." Justin sighs. Nicole chuckles pulling back. She smiles widely at us before she walks over to where Austin is sitting.

"I'll give you one." She smiles before hugging him tightly. By the looks of it the hug is much tighter than our hug.

"Thanks mom, but can't breath." He chokes.

"You wanted the hug." My mom laughs.

"This isn't what I meant." He coughs. Nicole lets him go taking her seat again.

"When is your sister coming home?" Justin asks Austin.

"She said this weekend. Also she found a boy." Austin says drying.

"Great." Justin says through clenched teeth.

"Good for her, that last one was suck a fuck boy." Nicole says. We all look to her with wide eyes. "Sorry, did I say something wrong?" She asks innocently. We all start laughing the tension I felt before evaporated.___
_______________________________________Hope you like it.

If you did please show it some love

What do we think of Austin?

Love you all

XO

Chapter eleven: facing school

To say I'm nervous is an understatement. I try walking down the school halls normally, but I feel everyone's eyes on me. I know no one is looking at me, but I can't help it. I'm stopped as someone grabs my shoulders making me tense. "Bee, it's me." Alex whispers in my ear. I let out a breath feeling myself relax. Alex turns me around to face him, and Chris and Nini come to join us.

"Hey, what's wrong?" Nini asks taking in my, probably, worried look. I look to Alex with wide eyes before looking to then.

"Can we talk to you two, after school?" Alex asks. They look to each other, with their own worried looks, and look back to us.

"Of course."

"Are you guys okay?" Chris asks. I smile at him nodding my head.

"Yeah, we are fine." I assure him. He nods his head looking to Alex. Alex nods his head agreeing that we are fine.

"Okay, where?"

"My house?" Alex offers.

"Okay, sounds good." Chris says, looking to his phone for the time. "We should probably get to our next class." We all groan in agreement. We each go our separate ways, Chris and I heading to the same class. "Bianca, can I ask you something?" I look to him raising an eyebrow.

"Do I look like I wouldn't listen?" He cracks a smile at that shaking his head.

"Okay then, do you think Nini has any feelings for me?" He rubs the back of his neck nervously.

"Why might you be asking?"

"Well..." He trails off. Our class is a few doors down making me groan.

"Do you like her?" I ask grabbing his arm, and looking at him in the eyes. His eyes widen as his cheeks tint a slight pink. "You do!" I exclaim. He covers my mouth making me quiet.

"Keep it down." He pleads.

"Sorry." I whisper. He pulls his hand away sighing.

"I do, but I don't want to make a move unless I know she has feelings for me." He explains. We walk into the room taking our seats. Chris sits behind me as we sit in the back by the windows.

"She does." I whisper as the bell rings. I can see his eyes widen, and he opens his mouth to speak only to close it. The teacher starts teach as the bell rings. I turn to face the front and ignore the boy behind me who has so much running through his head. I can feel him tapping my shoulder wanting me to turn around, but I keep looking straight ahead. When the bell finally rings I rush out of the class room before Chris can get to me.

"Hey bitch, we heard about you." One girl says. I stop in my tracks looking at her, my heart racing. She has brown hair and hazel eyes that seem to be fake. She probably wears different colored contacts.

"Who told you?" There is only one person that could have told about the baby, and that's Alex. She laughs at me, and her friends join in.

"The whole school knows about the fight." She sobers up. I let out a relived breath knowing she doesn't mean about the baby.

"Yeah, why were you the one that was let off the hook?" One of her friends sneer. Her hair is dyed red, which she has down in curls. Her brown eyes look at me like I am the grossest thing she has ever seen.

"I was defending myself." I point out. They scoff mumbling something under their breath as they walk away. I stand stunned by what just happened, but a hand makes me jump as it's placed on my shoulder.

"Bianca, are you okay?" I sigh hearing Nini's voice. My body longs for it to be Alex, but I'm happy it's one of my friends. I turn to look at her trying to look as normal as possible.

"Sure."

"B-"

"It has to do with what I need to tell you later." She nods her head understanding.

--

We are all siting down on the floor with the pillows and blankets ready for our movie night. It's Friday, and a great way to start the weekend is a movie night. We are at Alex's house in his finished basement. Austin is out, and Alex's parents are at my house with my parents. Chris and Nini look at us waiting for us to finally tell them what we need to tell them. I sigh looking for Alex, who automatically takes my hand in his. We look back to our friends nerves setting in.

"I'm pregnant." Their eyes widen as they look to Alex then to me before looking to each other. They look back to us, and Nini glances down towards my stomach. Chris's mouth drops as he scoots a little closer.

"Really?" He asks. I nod my head squeezing Alex's hand.

"And it's both of yours?" Nini voices in. We nod our heads stiffly.

"Dude, this is going to be fun." Chris grins.

"What do you mean?" I ask afraid of what Chris plans to do with my baby.

"I get to spoil this baby rotten. Well, once I get a better job that pays more." He adds. I laugh rolling my eyes.

"Are you showing yet?" Nini asks.

"It was just a conformation appointment, so it was too small to see." Alex says.

"Which means..." I roll my eyes at Chris.

"If you can't see the baby yet how could I be showing?" He still looks confused making me groan.

"Ugh dude, you are hopeless." Alex groans. Nini laughs shaking her head, and Chris looks to her frowning.

"I'm sorry I'm not that smart." He pouts.

"So, you guys don't hate us?" I voice. They both look to me confused as hell.

"Why the hell would we hate you?"

"The whole school will. I just wanted to make sure we had our best friend on our side." Nini frowns hugging me tight. I hug her back feeling tears prick my eyes.

"Way to go, Nini. You made her cry." Chris scolds.

"Chris, she has been crying a lot lately. Calm down." Alex states. I gasp pulling away from Nini.

"Have I really?" I choke out before sobbing. "I'm sorry I'm so emotional." I sob. Alex pulls me in his arms, and places me on his lap.

"Shh Bee, no one is mad at you. It wasn't meant to make you upset. I love you Bee I wouldn't say that to hurt you." He whispers in my ear. Goosebumps cover my neck, and down my body from his words from his breath on my neck.

"I'm sorry."

"Don't be." He kisses my collarbone making me shiver in pleasure.

"Guys, not while we are here." Chris groans.

"Yeah, please let's just start a movie." Nini begs.______________________
______________Hope you like it

If you did please show it some love

Love you all

XO

Chapter twelve: she is back

I hold onto my pillow more snuggling my head in more to hide from the light. I hear a groan from under me, but ignore it. My pillow starts to move, and I groan knowing it is Alex. "Stop moving." I plead.

"We have to get up." He tells me. "Come on you got to see this." He whispers in my ear. I open my eyes looking towards him. He nods his head to where he wants me to look. I look over to see Chris and Nini cuddling together as they sleep. A smile plays on my lips watching the two knowing they probably don't even realize it.

"Now I'm hungry." I pout as my stomach makes a loud noise demanding food. Alex chuckles nodding his head.

"You have to get off me first." He points out. I narrow my eyes at him not wanting to move.

"But I'm comfy and don't want to." I pout my lips more than before making Alex groan. His lips are then on mine making me gaps. I close my eyes kissing him back, and somehow when he pulls back I'm laying on my back as he hovers over me.

"I'll go start breakfast. Why don't you wake up those two." He smiles. I nod my head still dazed from the kiss. Alex kisses my lips once more quickly before he gets up. I lay there for a minute having reality come back to me. Looking over to my sleeping friends, I grab the pillow next to me as I sit up before throwing it at them. They stir and groan as the pillow hit them in the face. I watch them smiling as their eyes open. Nini turns over her eyes widening as hers meet Chris's.

"Come on you two, Alex started breakfast." With that I get up skipping to the stairs. I hurry up them wanting food. I skip to the kitchen and make my way to the counter before hopping on it. Alex raises an eyebrow at me as he watches mixing pancake mix together.

"Where are they?"

"They should be coming up." I say looking over my shoulder to watch them walk awkwardly in the kitchen.

"Morning. Hey, do you guys want chocolate chip pancakes?" Alex asks.

"Yes!" We all shout together. Alex shakes his head laughing as he grabs the packet of chocolate chips.

"Do you parents know about the baby?" Chris asks leaning against the counter by the stove facing me.

"Yeah, they all do. The only one who doesn't is Olivia." Alex answers for us.

"How is she doing?" Nini asks leaning on the island by me. She is slumped over in the chair just watching Alex cook.

"Good I guess. She should be coming home today."

"I can't wait to see her." I grin. Alex shoots me a look over his shoulder.

"She might kill me though." Alex says. I laugh at him, and so do Chris and Nini.

"True she always has been the protective one over Bianca." Chris tries to sober up. I only grin wider in agreement.

"It shouldn't be too bad." Nini says.

"True. Austin seemed pretty chill with it." I point out.

"When you left he threatened me to never leave you or the baby. Not that I would anyway." He adds at the end.

"See Austin knows things." Chris smiles. I roll my eyes at him as I watch Alex flip the pancake on a plate.

"Yeah. Who knew he could be serious." I look to Nini smiling at her words, and I can hear Alex let out a snort. The front door opens with a groan making all of us look to see who it is. Olivia drags herself in towing a bag behind her. She tries to look to us smiling, but you can tell how tired she really is.

"Hey guys." She yawns. Alex leaves the stove letting Chris take over. He hugs Olivia tightly, and she matches his hug back. I smile at the two siblings happy she is back.

"Hey sis, you should go get some rest." Alex says kissing her cheek. She smiles at him pulling away from the hug.

"Will do, talk to you guys later." She waves before hurrying up the stairs. Alex turns to us still smiling.

"Well, this should be fun." I can't help but grin at his words.

"Great, now can you please finish breakfast? I'm starving." I whine. Alex kisses my lips quick on his way to the stove.

"Give me five minutes." He tells me.

"But I'm hungry now." I pout.

"Awe look at the little baby." Chris coos. I glare at him crossing my arms over my chest. "Is she going to throw a tantrum?" He asks in a cute voice as if talking to a child.

"Chris, just stop. You don't want to make it worse." Nini scolds him.

"Yeah, then I have to save your ass." Alex shoots turning off the stove.

"Wow, really feeling the love." I state hopping off the island as I feel a tear fall down my cheek. I walk away to the bathroom to calm myself down. I can hear them all arguing about who actually set me off. I blame the hormones because that's how we usually talk to each other.

"Bianca, is that you in there?" I jump at Olivia's voice. I look to see her peeking through the crack of the door I left open.

"Yeah, what's up?" I sniffle wiping my tears away. She comes in sighing as she takes in my watery eyes.

"Why are you crying? What did they say to you? I'll give them a piece of my mind." She starts as she holds my shoulders. Her arms start to rub up and down my arms comforting me.

"I'll tell you, but promise me you won't get mad." I tell her. I know I have to tell her the truth. Alex should probably be here too for telling her about the baby, but I think now is the best time. I know she won't stop with questions until she gets an actual answer.

"Okay, I promise." She sighs. Her eyes try to read mine to try and understand what is going on.

"I'm pregnant."

"Who is the father?"

"Alex." She raises an eyebrow at me.

"My brother Alex?" I nod my head bitting my lip trying to read her. She just seems frozen stunned by the news.

"Olivia?"

"Are you kidding?"

"No." Her hands stop as they just grip my shoulders.

"When? Are you even together?"

"Yes, we have been for a bit now. Before we found out." She just nods her head taking in the information.

"He better not leave your ass, if he tries you let me know. I'll beat the shit out of him." She warns. I crack a smile at that knowing she isn't mad.

"You and Austin." I chuckle.

"Austin knows?"

"Yeah, so do our parents, Chris, Nini, and my siblings." I tell her. She nods her head letting go of me.

"Why was I the last to know?" She pouts.

"We wanted to tell you in person." Alex opens the door, and freezes looking between the two of us.

"Breakfast is ready." He says looking to Olivia as she glares at him. "You told her?" He asks looking to me.

"I kinda had to." He rolls his eyes walking away. We both follow after him, me going for the food and Olivia yelling at him. I feel bad I told her without him, and I know he isn't happy with it. "Olivia, stop. Alex I'm sorry." She groans walking away. Alex looks to me shrugging, but I know he wants to say something.____Hope you like it

If you did please show it some love

Do you think she messed up? Or is Alex over reacting?

Love you all

XO

Chapter thirteen: great... just great

I bite my lip watching him pace his bedroom as I sit in his bed. I feel bad about telling Olivia without him, and I know he is pissed. "Alex, I'm sorry. I didn't want to, but you know how she is." He stops pacing looking to me with narrow eyes.

"Yes I know how she is, but that didn't give you the right. We agreed to do it together." He tries not to shout. I gulp not liking him acting like this. He is right though, I did mess up. I close my eyes feeling the tears leave them.

"I'm sorry, Alex." I open my eyes to meet his angry ones. "I really am." I whisper before forcing myself up. I hurry out of his house running to the safety of my own. As soon as I reach mine I sprint to my room slamming the door shut. I fall on my bed as the sobs come through. I faintly hear my door open, but ignore it.

"Honey, what's wrong?" My mom's gentle voice comes through. I hold back a sob turning my head to look up at her. She rubs her hand soothingly on my back.

"I think Alex hates me." I choke out.

"Why?" Her eyebrows furrow as confusion washes over her features.

"I told Olivia without him. She kinda cornered me wanting to know what was up because I was crying, and I just told her."

"Shh baby." She tires to calm me as she hugs me bringing me closer to her. I look up to see my dad at my door, and he is fuming.

"What did he do?" I shake my head sobbing. I nuzzle my head into my mom's shoulder wanting her comfort like when I was young. I can hear him storm away, but I can't seem to care.

"Mom, what's up with Bianca?" Tony asks. I look up to see my worried siblings taking cautious steps into my room.

"It's Okay. Bianca just feels like she messed up, but she didn't." Kait comes up and hops on my bed joining the hug.

"Don't worry Bee. It all works out in the end." She tries to assure me. I can't help but smile at my little sister. I kiss her cheek hugging her tight.

"Thank you, sis." I grin letting her go to wipe my tears. Tony clears his throat making me look to him.

"Bee, I highly doubt you could have messed anything up. You are the only one I know that can only fix things." He tells me. I reach out to hug him making him groan, but I sneak a kiss on his cheek anyway.

"Thanks bud." I ruffle his hair before he could step back. He runs his hands through it trying to fix it.

"So, when can we see a picture of the baby?" Kait asks breaking the silence. I feel them all look at me as I glance down to my stomach.

"My next appointment in a few weeks. Would you want to come?" I ask her. She grins looking to our mom.

"Mom, can I?" My mom smiles nodding her head.

"As long as I get to go." I smile laughing lightly. I love my family, and for them to make me smile instead of crying. I know I can count on them for anything. I don't know what will do happen at school when I start to show, but I know my family can make it all better.

--

I walk into school without Alex by my side, which breaks my heart a little. I was scared to talk to him after the argument, so I've been ignoring him a little. I want to make sure he has settled down all the way before I see him. I get to the hall my locker is in and stop dead in my tracks. Alex is there leaning against my locker with his arms crossed over his chest. His black shirt is fitted so you can get a preview of what his abs look like, and the shirt sleeves show his muscular arms. Damn this boy. He is also wearing khakis, which makes a smile find its way on my face. I keep walking watching him, and he must feel my eyes as he looks up. His eyes meet mine, and a smile graces his lips.

"Morning Bee." Alex chimes pushing himself off my locker, and wrapping his arms around me. I melt into his embrace not being able to stay stone cold.

"Alex." I sigh looking up into his eyes. Regret and pain flash through his eyes surprising me.

"I'm so sorry, Bee." He starts, hugging me tight against him. "I overreacted, and I shouldn't have. I really didn't mean to get mad at you, I'm sorry. Please don't leave me. I need to be in my baby's life." He whispers the last part in my ear. Tears already fall down my face from his words. I pull back wiping them along with blaming these stupid hormones.

"It's okay, Alex." I assure him. He raises an eyebrow still unsure. He still seems to be full of the regret making me frown. "What?"

"Nothing." He rushes. My eyebrows furrow together wondering what he is hiding. I shrug my shoulders moving around him to get to my locker.

"Hey, Alex!" We both turn to see some guy from the basketball team. He looks at me with clear disgust making me bite my lip. I look down at my outfit, which is a pair of Alex's Adidas pants with a navy blue tee shirt. I'm wearing my Nike trainers, and my hair is thrown in a bun. I know I didn't try at all today with it being Monday, I didn't even put makeup on.

"Don't look at my girl like that." Alex snaps, making the guy look to him. His eyes are wide as Alex takes a step closer to my side.

"Dude, are you kidding? She is a nobody. You really picked her?" He seems appalled that Alex could even think about that. In our school basketball and soccer are the top two sports, so the players should be seen with the cheerleaders. Alex isn't like that and neither is Chris, they find it down right repulsive.

"Dude, if you don't start showing my girl some respect you are going to have a problem." Alex threatens. The guy rolls his eyes at Alex as he crosses his arms over his chest.

"And what are you going to do about it?"

"Teach you a lesson." Alex shrugs.

"How, dumbass?" Alex sigh stepping towards the guy. Alex is just a few inches taller than him giving him the upper hand.

"Well, see I would punch you right here right now, but that would cause problems for my position on the team." Alex's voice is low and cold. I've never seen this side to him, and honestly I don't know if I like it or if I absolutely hate it. They other guy gets pissed as his jaw clenches, but he relaxes smirking at Alex.

"What a coward." He mutters under his breath before he turns to leave. Alex tenses and before I know it he grabs the guy's arm making him turn back to face himself, and Alex punches him right in the jaw. I gasp blinking my wide eyes as I watch them now wrestling on the floor.

Well isn't this great.____Hope you liked it

If you did please show it some love

Thought?

Love you all

XO

Chapter fourteen: the first picture

I sit in study hall working on some homework I know I won't get to. I have a doctor appointment today to get an ultrasound, and my mom and sister are going with me. Alex really wants to, but he has practice. After he got in a fight with that kid, Jack, his coach has been on his case about everything. So, I told him he needs to go to get on the coaches good side. I glance up to see Chris take a seat in front of me, and I raise an eyebrow at him.

"Shouldn't you been in class right now?" He shrugs watching me finish the sentence I am finishing writing. "What's up?" I ask giving him my full attention.

"So, I want to ask Nini out." I squeal in excitement. He ignores me continuing what he wants to say. "I don't know how though, and I want to do it soon." I just watch him nervously run an hand through his hair as I grin like a crazy person.

"All you got to do is sit down with her and talk to her. You know before it's too late, and one of you just stops talking to the other for no reason." Chris raises an eyebrow at home.

"And, you have gone through this?"

"Eh, but stop we are talking about your love life."

"What do you mean eh?"

"Ugh," I groan. "I stopped talking to Alex for no reason whatsoever. Somehow he came out and confronted me, but we all know Nini won't do that."

"Okay, I didn't mean to poke the beast." He raises his hands in surrender. I sigh looking back down to my work. "So I should just sit down and talk to her?"

"Yup." I chirp looking up to him. He smiles at me nodding his head as he thinks about it. His eyes show hesitation making me sigh. "Chris, if you want her, go get her." I flat out tell him.

"You're right." He smiles. He stands up groaning as he checks the time on his phone. "I got to go back to class. See you later." He walks off, and I start back on my work. I smile knowing my friends will be together soon, and will stop coming to me about their doubts on each other's feelings.

--

We walk home all smiling as I look back to the ultrasound picture in my hands. I smile at my little baby that is growing inside me. I stop as two strong arms wrap around me, and a kiss is placed on my neck. "Is that our little bean?" Alex asks excitedly. I smile glancing to his face that is lit up with totally happiness.

"Oh Alex you should have seen it!" Kait exclaims. Alex lets me go looking to my sister, who feels like she just witnessed the best thing in the world. My mom smiles at her looking to Alex as she shuts the door.

"I wish I was there, kiddo." Alex sighs. Kait shrugs before she heads to the kitchen. She mutters something about getting food before she dies.

"Alex, don't be hard on yourself for it. There will be more ultrasounds." My mom says patting his shoulder as she walks by. Alex lets out a breath, and I can see him still downing himself. I turn towards him and wrap my arms around him in a hug. He hugs me back burying his head in the crook of my neck.

"Hey, our little bean is healthy. Alex please don't worry." I plead not wanting him to feel bad.

"But I missed the appointment." He mumbles against my skin. I sigh resting my head against his.

"Alex, it is totally fine. You will be there for the next one, and every appointment after that." I tell him. He pulls back, and looks to me analyzing my eyes with his.

"What if I have practice?"

"I made the next one early, so we will just go into school late." I tell him. He grins at me kissing my lips.

"So, I get to see our little bean." He smiles placing a hand on my lower stomach. I smile kissing his cheek, which makes him look to me. His lips meet mine, and I can feel his smile on them.

"Okay you two. That's enough." I hear my dad clear his throat. We jump apart looking to my dad. He stares Alex down before looking to me grinning. "Can I see the ultrasound picture?" I grin back nodding my head. I give him the picture, which he takes eagerly.

"Alex, your family is coming over for dinner tonight." My mom says slipping pass us to walk upstairs.

"What time?" I ask, which stops her on the stairs.

"They will be here in an hour." She says as she starts walking again.

"What the hell are we going to be eating?" My dad asks walking up after her, but not before giving me the picture back. I shake my head heading to the kitchen. I feel Alex follow me until we are in the room alone. His arms are suddenly around me, and turn me to face him. His lips then are on mine in a second making me melt. My legs turn to jello making me grip onto Alex's biceps. My eyes close as the kiss fills with passion. Our lips move together perfectly as they claim each other's. His tongue licks my bottom lip wanting entry, which I hesitate to grant. Everyone is home! If someone walks in we would be dead.

Being in his arms, though, and having his lips on mine my mind becomes cloudy. Hearing footsteps come closer I force us to pull apart, and I open the fridge to grab a water. I hear Alex chuckle behind me, I shut the fridge shooting him a glare as I open the water bottle. "Thirsty?" He asks. My eyes widen at his question making him laugh harder. "You are so red right now." He grins. I groan turning around, taking a sip of my water.

"Kids, why don't you go outside and do something?" My mom says walking into the kitchen.

"Tony, Kait lets go play a game." Alex says loudly, which gets them to come running.

"What are we playing?" Tony asks excitedly. I turn around to watch them. Alex grins at him, and looks to Kait too.

"What do you want to play?"

"Soccer!" They cheer. Alex laughs nodding his head.

"Then lets go." He turns around to watch them run into the backyard. I he looks to me, and grins.

"Can I play?" I ask. He frowns at me shaking his head. He walks up to me, and caresses my face.

"I'm sorry, Bee. I don't want you playing. We can't have you getting hurt, and something happening." I frown at him. He gives me a pointed look making me sigh.

"Okay, just don't go to hard on them." I warn him. He grins at me kissing my lips quick.

"I know what to do." With that he runs out. I feel my mom come stand next to me as she laughs.

"He is just like his father." I look to her raising an eyebrow. "Don't look so surprised. Same with your father, except he barely changed." I laugh at that.____Hope you liked it. Sorry for the late update, time just got the best of me. The next one won't take as long.

Please show it some love

Love you all

XO

Please check out my new story His Angel

Chapter fifteen: scared

I t's Alex and Chris' first game of the basketball season. Nini and I can't contain our excitement for watching them play. Chris and Nini have had their talk, and apparently after the game they are going out on a date. Nini and I grab our seats on the bleachers close to the court wanting to see our guys play. The whole gym is packed with students and families from both teams. Suddenly the announcer starts talking and everyone quiets down. The visiting team comes out getting cheers from their school. When our team comes out our side screams for our players. My eyes lock on Alex as soon as he enters the gym. He finds my eyes grinning at me, and I can't help but grin back.

We watch them warm up before the game actually starts. Nini and I watch the game in awe as our two boys are playing, and surprisingly they are really good. Apparently they are both amazing at basketball and soccer. I watch as our team makes a basket before our whole side erupts with cheers. Honestly I don't know how this game is totally played. I only really know soccer.

The game was won 27-24. Alex runs up to me and wraps his arms around me. I groan as he holds me against his sweaty body. "Alex, go shower." I groan out trying to push him.

"What, no kiss first?" He pouts. I raise an eyebrow at him making him let me go. "Fine, I'll be back in a few." He then runs off to shower.

"Wow, you got him whipped." I hear an annoying voice say. I glare up at her, Claire, the head cheerleader. Her hair is dark brown with highlights that have to be recently done, and her brown eyes glare into my eyes.

"What are you doing?"

"You think you can take my man from me?" Nini bursts out laughing.

"Oh hun that's cute." She tries to sober up.

"Don't talk, bitch."

"Aye! Don't talk to my friend that way." I shout. Claire narrows her eyes on me.

"I do what I want. Now, leave Alex before he breaks your heart for me. That's probably the nicest warning I have ever done." She says. I laugh at her words making her face turn red in anger.

"He won't leave me for your sorry ass. He wouldn't be able to live with himself if he left me for you." She shoves me pushing me to the ground. I stay there wishing I didn't just hurt my baby. Nini's eyes are wide as she looks at me.

"Don't say that! He is mine, and will be mine!" She shouts. Nini rolls her eyes before throwing a punch to Claire's nose, and I can hear it break. I just stay on the ground with tears in my eyes. My heart races as I face the ground that is just inches from my face.

"What the fuck?" I hear Chris. I look up to him with my wide eyes as tears start to leak through.

"Go get Alex." I whisper. He runs off to find Alex as Nini squats down to my level.

"We have to move you, hun." I shake my head as more tears flow.

"I'm too scared." No one seems to be paying attention as everyone leaves the gym.

"I know, but we have to move you." She tells me gently. I shake my head too afraid to. What if something happened? I hear sneakers squeaking on the court making me look up to see Alex running to me. He looks just as worried as I do. He gets down to my level worry seeping through his pores.

"Bee, what happened?" He asks trying to seem calm.

"Claire." I get out before I bite my lip to not start sobbing.

"She fucking pushed you? We will deal with her later, come on lets get you checked." He says. He stands up before he bends down to pick me up. He carries me bridal style out of the gym, and straight to the nurse.

"What if she isn't in there?" Chris asks leading the way.

"Then we will go to the doctors, we need something- someone." Alex panics. We get to the nurse's office, which is luckily still open. Alex rushes me in making the nurse jump in surprise.

"Oh my. What seems to be the problem?" She asks coming over as Alex rests me on the little bed thing in here.

"She was pushed to the ground." Alex tells as if that summed up the whole thing. She gives him a look raising an eyebrow.

"She's pregnant." Chris adds. That seems to clear it up for her as she starts to check me out.

"How did you land?"

"My side."

"Any bleeding?"

"No."

"Pain or discomfort in your abdominal regain?"

"No. I'm just scared."

"I know honey. From what I can tell everything seems to be fine. How far are you?"

"Three months." She nods her head smiling.

"You should be fine. If it was farther along I would worry more, but you and the baby seem to be fine."

"Thank you." I grin.

"If you ever need anything during the school day just come on down." She tells me.

--

Alex holds me as we lay on his bed. It feels good to know nothing is wrong, but it still scares me that anything can happen. His door opens slowly before Austin comes in, and by how he is sneaking in its big. "Austin?" He shuts the door before sitting on the bed facing us.

"I need to tell you guys something." He says carefully. Alex and I share a look before we look to a nervous Austin.

"What is it?"

"I'm engaged." He whispers. My eyes widen as I sit straight up.

"To who? I thought you aren't dating anyone." Alex says sitting straight up.

"I know, I wanted to keep it on the down low. We have only been dating for six months, but we love each other. Like you two love each other." I can see it in his eyes that he means it.

"As long as you love each other, but you have to tell your parents." I smile. Austin groans not liking the sound of that.

"I got your back, bro." Alex says putting a hand on his shoulder. Austin gives us a small smile, and I pull him in for a hug.

"Congrats, but I want to meet her." I say. Austin chuckles.

"She is coming next weekend." He grins.

"Why did you tell us?" Alex voices.

"I need to hear some feed back, and I knew you two would understand."
_______________________________________Hope you liked it

If you did please show it some love

Love you all

XO

Chapter sixteen: Austin's girl

- -

I watch out the window waiting for the car to pull up. Austin told Alex and I to be at the house when he got home. He is bringing his fiancée to visit the family, and tell them about the engagement. Right now it is only Alex, Koda, and I in the house. Olivia is still in her last class before she can leave, and their parents are at work. Alex sighs flipping through the channels trying to find something good to watch. "Aren't you anxious?" I look at him to see him shrug.

"Should I be?" I roll my eyes at him flopping on the couch next to him. He wraps his arm around me pulling me closer to him as a smile plays on his lips.

"What if your parents disown him? What would you do?" Alex rolls his eyes at me.

"Bee, they would have disowned me. They aren't like that." I sigh resting my head on his shoulder.

"I'm sorry."

"Why are you sorry?"

"I got us into this situation."

"Bee," he sighs, "we have gone over this. It takes two to make a baby." He pulls me to sit on his lap. "I blame me for wanting you all the damn time. Maybe we should have waited longer." I shake my head cupping his face in my hands.

"Alex, stop. It was not your fault. I wanted you just as much as you wanted me. I don't regret it though, you know giving myself to you." He smiles at me. His kisses my lips just as a car honks their horn. We both look to the window to see Austin's car in the driveway.

"I guess we should go and greet them." Alex says. I grin jumping off his lap, and rushing out the door. I can hear him laughing behind me as he tries to catch up. I run right to Austin, who wraps me in a big hug. I hug him back grinning like crazy.

"I'm so happy you are here." He chuckles letting me go. He looks behind me to Alex, and nods in acknowledgment.

"Bro, you should keep your girl close to you, and away from sugar." Austin smiles. I narrow my eyes at him as Alex laughs.

"Austin, be nice to her." A girl says coming to stand next to Austin. He looks to her grinning as he wraps an arm around her. You can see the love in his eyes as he looks to her, and she looks to him with the same look.

"I'm sorry babe, but it's only Bianca. I've known her since she was born." She rolls her eyes at him looking to Alex and I.

"Hi, I'm Holly." She smiles. She has blonde hair that flows in natural waves over her shoulders. Her eyes are shining bright blue, which show nothing but care and kindness. I smile at her leaning into Alex's chest.

"I'm Bianca, and this is Alex." She laughs at my words making my eyebrows furrow.

"Austin told me who you are, and showed me pictures of you guys. Congratulations by the way." I can only smile at her feeling Alex's arms wrap around me.

"Thank you." Alex says for us. "Come on, why don't we go inside."

"Alex, help me with our bags." Austin says heading to the back of his car. Alex groans, but listens. He kisses my cheek before he goes to the trunk. I lead Holly into the house excitedly.

"So, right now no one else is here?" She asks taking in the silence.

"Nope, oh wait. Koda is outside." I say heading to the kitchen wanting some fruit. She follows me looking out the back door. Koda is sleeping on the deck, and I can hear her awe over him.

"So, how did your family take it?" I ask as she comes towards me. I hop on the island as she leans against the counter.

"I don't have a family, so I had no one to tell." I frown at her words. "I was in foster care for as long as I could remember. When I turned 18 they let me go."

"I'm so sorry." She shakes her head smiling.

"Don't be, that's in the past. How do you think his parents will take it?" She asks, nervousness clear in her voice.

"I wouldn't worry too much. I mean Alex and I are having a baby."

"Olivia is on her way home." Alex announces walking into the room. He comes over to me smiling, and opening his mouth. I put a grape on his mouth making his smile as he chews it. His kisses my lips quick before stepping back as Austin clears his throat.

"Bro, please don't be all lovey dovey around us. That's all I ask." I roll my eyes at him.

"So-"

"Should we go then?" Alex asks raising an eyebrow.

"No, bro I need you here. You promised."

"Then don't get on my case. I'm surprised you aren't like this." Holly starts laughing as she hugs Austin.

"Are you kidding? This goof is just holding back." I watch as Austin's cheeks turn a hint of pink making me smile, and Alex chuckle. Suddenly the door opens, and we hear their parents come in.

"Kids?" Nicole calls.

"In the kitchen." Austin responds.

"Bianca." Justin smiles as he sees me, and Nicole grins at me taking me into a hug, after I hopped off the counter.

"Hi, who are you? I'm Austin and Alex's mom, Nicole, and this is Justin, their dad." Nicole greets her with a warm smile. Holly looks to Austin for help, and he wraps his arm around her smiling to his mom.

"Mom, this is Holly my fiancée." Nicole stands there shocked looking to Justin before they look back to Austin and Holly.

"Son, why didn't you say anything?" Justin asks.

"It just happened. We just fell deeply in love, and I can't live without her." Austin says looking to Holly. And his eyes shine with the truth behind his words.

"Well, welcome to the family." Nicole grins hugging Holly and Austin. Justin joins the hug, and so do Alex and I.

"Olivia is going to be so jealous she is the last to hear." Justin says.

"Too bad." Nicole shrugs. This is why I love their parents. We laugh breaking away from the hug. "So, what do we want for dinner?" Nicole asks heading to the fridge.

"Whatever is good for me." Justin says.

"Bianca, got any cravings?" I laugh shaking my head.

"Nope, just hungry." She laughs looking in the fridge.

"How about I make some pasta? Is that good with you kids?"

"Yes." We all agree. This should be a good night, or at least until Olivia comes and gets pissed for knowing last._

Hope you liked it!

If you did please show it some love

Love you all

XO

Chapter seventeen: wanting out

Two months later

"I hate this. It's so obvious now. How can I hide it?" Alex cups my face in his hands. I lock my eyes with his, and everything disappears.

"You will be fine. So what if people notice? Fuck them." I roll my eyes at him. "You are coming to the game right?"

"The last one/ senior one? Yes, I am. I can't believe basketball is done all ready." I say. Alex smiles kissing my lips.

"Me neither. Now, lets walk into school." I groan. Alex chuckles letting my face go as he takes my right hand in his left one. I look down to my noticeable pregnant belly. Alex told me not to worry because I look beautiful, but at month 5 there is no way of hiding it now. We walk through the halls, and I can feel the eyes on me and the whispers. I bite my lip as we reach my locker, and I can feel Nini and Chris come up to us. I look to them to see their hands are interlocked, which makes me smile. They have been together officially for a month now, and couldn't be happier.

"Good morning you two." Nini grins.

"Someone got laid." Alex smirks. Nini blushes a bright red looking down to the floor and Chris just rolls his eyes.

"You ready for the game?"

"Ready as I'll ever be." Alex smiles. I lean into his side as his arm wraps around me. I look up to him meeting his eyes, which sparkle at me.

"Fucking slut." Someone mutters as he walks pass us. I can feel my heart squeeze from their words, and Alex squeezes me a little tighter reassuringly. I can feel my eyes become watery, but I refuse to let tears fall before lunch.

"Aye asshole!" Chris shouts. The guy turns back glaring at Chris.

"What?"

"You know what. Keep your filthy mouth shut." Chris warns. I hide into Alex's side not liking this confrontation. The guy looks Chris over before looking to Alex and I. His eyebrows furrow as our eyes connect.

"Why, Chris are you the baby daddy? Did you two fuck and keep it a secret? That explains why you guys have been talking every study hall." The guy smirks at me before he walks off. Nini looks between Chris and I, and Alex does the same. He looks me in the eyes frowning seeing the tears.

"Bee?" Alex whispers. I shake my head tears slipping out, and my heart breaking.

"Alex I wouldn't, I couldn't." He sighs hugging me close against him. He mumbles that he believes me and he knows neither of us would sleep behind the others' backs. Chris wouldn't be able to even think like that about me because of how much he has always liked Nini.

"I know, I know. Its okay Bee, but we have to get to class." I take deep breathes calming down as his words sink in. He is right we have to carry on with the day. I pull away from him only to get a kiss on my forehead.

"Come on, guys. Lets go start the longest day of school." Nini says trying to stay positive.

--

"And here I was the one to believe this wouldn't happen between your two." AJ sighs sitting across from me in art. Jack sits next to him all smug, which makes me raise an eyebrow. "Ignore him, he won a bet." I snap my eyes to AJ stunned.

"You bet on us?" They both laugh at that smiling, but AJ stops seeing my hurt expression.

"Honey, everyone has been making bets." Jack smiles.

"Why?"

"Do you really have to ask? Come on, Alex's parents had Austin and Olivia at your age. If it didn't happen to them it was bound to happen to Alex." AJ speaks easily.

"Plus your parents had you young." I shake my head standing up.

"Bianca, is there a problem?" I hear the teacher. I look into his judgmental eyes, and can't help the tears leak from mine. I run out of the art room, and head straight for the nurse's office. I step in, and meet her eyes immediately. She puts down her cup of coffee coming to me.

"Honey, what is wrong?" I break down in front of her, and she takes me into her arms. She walks me a little way before I feel her reach for something. "Hi, yes. Can you send Alex down to the nurse's office. Thank you." With that I feel her hand reach again before they both rub my back. "It's okay honey." She tries to reassure.

"I don't want to be here anymore." I sob into her shoulder.

"Whats wrong?" I hear Alex's voice in a panic, and slightly out of breath.

"She just came to me crying." The nurse tells him. I pull away from her as I feel Alex's hands on my body. I turn to him, and into his embrace as his arms move to wrap around me tightly.

"Whats wrong Bee?"

"I don't want to be here anymore."

"What do you mean?"

"School." I choke out.

"We will talk about this later with our parents, but for now lets get you home." I nod my head, and he sighs before he picks me up carrying me out.

"Okay." I whisper.

"Thank you." I hear Alex tell the nurse before he walks out of the room. The bell rings letting everyone into the hall, and I can feel the eyes on Alex and I. I don't care as much because I refuse to come back to this place. The cold air hits my skin making me shiver, but I welcome it. Christmas is in a week, and I can't wait. There is a part of me that is scared though, Alex's uncle hasn't seen us since the pregnancy, but I'm sure he was told. Alex sits me in his car and shuts the door. He gets in the car sighing as he starts it up.

"Alex?" I voice wiping the tears from my cheeks.

"Yes."

"Are you mad at me?" He glances at me quick before looking to the road.

"Why on earth would I be mad at you?"

"The game, and all this other shit."

"Bee, stop with that. Don't think like that, and for your question- no. I'm not mad at you, I fucking love you. We will still go to the game, or at least I will. I don't want to force you to go back to the school." His hand moves to grip my thigh, and I smile looking at his hand.

"I love you too." I whisper.

"What was that? I didn't catch it." He says amused. I roll my eyes before reaching to place a kiss on his cheek.

"I love you."___________________________________Hope you liked it

If you did please show it some love

Sorry if it seemed shitty I'm trying to work on that

Love you all

XO

Chapter eighteen: test found

Alex walks out of my bathroom that connects to my room with a puzzled look on his face. I raise an eyebrow as I watch him walk over to me. "What?"

"Why did you only just throw away the test?"

"What the hell are you talking about?" He looks to me furrowing his eyebrows together.

"The test." He says wanting me to understand. "The pregnancy test." I cock my head to the side my eyebrows furrowing in confusion.

"What do you mean? I got rid of that after telling you."

"Then why is there a positive one in your garbage?"

"What?" I ask getting off my bed, and heading into the bathroom. I look in the trash to see the test in there facing up. The positive sign on clear view to whoever were to glance that way. "What the hell?" I walk back out, and pace my room.

"It isn't yours?" I shake my head trying to think back to when someone was able to go in there and take it. Kait was home sick today, but Nini also went in their earlier before she went out with Chris. I look to Alex my heart racing as my thoughts go back to Kait. She is too young to be a mother, younger than me. Alex wraps his arms around me making me feel safe.

"Who's could it be?"

"I don't know. Kait was home sick from school today. Alex what if she is pregnant?" I whisper as I nuzzle my head into his chest.

"Shh, breathe Bee. I don't think it would be hers. Who else used it?"

"Nini."

"Maybe its Nini."

"She wasn't in there for a long enough time. I need to talk to Kait." I pull away from him before walking towards the door. Alex stops me as he grabs my arm.

"Let me do it. If she is really sick I don't want you to catch it." He says. I smile at him nodding my head.

"Thank you." Alex kisses my cheek before leaving my room. I smile watching him go to her room, and my stomach growls. I head to the kitchen craving some chocolate covered in peanut butter. I see my mom in there searching through the cabinets for something to eat before she grabs some chips. She walks over to the fridge opening it to grab the whipped cream. I raise an eyebrow as she puts some on the chip before eating it. She looks to me with wide eyes as if she has been caught.

"Um I can explain." She starts her mouth full. I roll my eyes grabbing the peanut butter and the chocolate chips.

"Can you?" She nods her head swallowing.

"It's really good." She tells me before doing that to another chip and eating it.

"I'm going to pass on that." I tell her as I take a spoon.

"What are you guys eating?" I hear my dad's confused voice.

"Just satisfying some cravings." I tell him digging the spoon into the peanut butter. He looks to my mom before looking back to me.

"Where is Alex."

"Right here." Alex answers walking into the kitchen, and coming to stand next to me. "I got to get going though. Austin needs help with moving some things in his room to fit his bigger bed." I nod my head sighing as I put the spoon in my mouth. "I'll see you later Bee." He smiles kissing my cheek before he leaves waving to my parents.

"Well then, let's start dinner." My mom sighs. "Babe, go pick Tony up form practice." She orders. My dad Brian's before grabbing his keys. "We have to tell you guys something at dinner." She tells me as she moves to get ingredients out for dinner.

--

We all sit at the table eating dinner happily, and I'm just waiting for them to tell us what they want to. I don't look to Kait even though I feel her eyes on me. "Okay, kids. We have to tell you all something." We all look to our parents waiting. What do they want to tell us? Wait is the test my mom's?

"We are hosting Christmas Eve at our house this year." My mom squeals. I let out a relieved breath out knowing they aren't having another kid. That means it has to be Kait's then.

"So we need to get the house ready in a day?" I ask.

"Yup." My dad grins.

"Why? It's always at Alex's house." Tony wonders.

"His mom has been feeling a little worn out lately, and wondered if we could take over." Our mom explains. My eyebrows furrow as the words sink in about Alex's mom.

"Is she okay?"

"She is fine, don't you worry." Our dad assures us.

"Are you sure?" Kait asks.

"Yes, now don't worry about it." Our mom assures. I continue eating making a mental note to as Alex about her. Once we are all finished Tony and I clean up the table as Katie trails back up to her room.

"What does Kait have?" I ask him as I put a plate in the dishwasher.

"A cold? I don't know. She had a temperature this morning, so mom kept her home." I nod my head letting out a breath of relief.

"Aww that sucks. Do you know how she is now? Alex doesn't want me to catch anything because of the baby."

"I get it. She is better now, just tired." I nod my head finishing putting the last dish in.

"I have to go talk to mom and dad, can you please finish up here?" I give him puppy dog eyes making Tony roll his eyes before he nods his head. "Thank you." I grin before talking out of the kitchen. My right hand subconsciously rests on my defined pregnant belly. I take a deep breath as I walk in on them talking in the family room. They jump looking to me, and share a look with each other.

"What's wrong?" I ask taking a cautious step.

"Nothing, honey. What's up?" My dad asks looking to me now. Their full attention was on me making me take a deep breath before letting it out.

"I don't want to go to school anymore."

"Why?" My mom's voice is concerned. I can feel tears prick my eyes stinging them.

"What have they been doing?" My dad asks.

"They call me names, give dirty looks. I just can't." I feel the tears slip free now, and I can see through my blurry eyes that my mom is crying too.

"It's okay honey. You can do online schooling. I won't have you go through that everyday." My mom says through her crying voice.

"I'm going to call that school of yours up." My dad grumbles under his breath. I shake my head feeling my tears streaming down. My mom gets up wrapping her arms around me.

"Even some teachers give me looks." I choke on her shoulder. My mom tries to soothe me as she rubs my back, and whispers sweet nothings. I don't flinch hearing the door open, and someone walks into the house. I know who it is, and by the sound of his voice I feel my body calm even more.

"What happened?" Worry laces his voice as I feel him walk closer to me.

"Fucking people at school." My dad spits. I can tell he is pissed, and there is no doubt he will say something to the school.

"Bee," Alex tries. My mom lets me go, and Alex takes her place. His arms hold me in a tight protective way making me feel safe. I rest my head on his shoulder just letting my tears run out. "It's okay, I got you." He whispers before kissing my head.____
_Hope you liked it

If you did please show some love

Love you all

XO

Chapter 19: christmas

I groan looking in my closet seeing nothing to wear. I sit on my bed just looking into my closet seeing nothing worthy of Christmas Eve. Alex dries his hair with his towel walking into the room. He wears kakis that hang low on his waist allowing the rim of his boxers to show. He wears no shirt right now letting his muscular body be on display. I advert my eyes back to my closet after seeing him smirk. "What's wrong, Bee?"

"I have nothing to wear." I pout. He takes the towel throwing it towards the bathroom before looking at me. He raises an eyebrow at me cocking his head to the side.

"You have a full closet. How is that possible?"

"Then you find something." I cross my arms over my chest annoyed. Alex smiles shaking his head as he stands up. I watch him walk to my closet look in it for a minute before pulling out an outfit. He pulls out black stretchy pants and a dark red sweater. He turns around and hands them to me.

"Are you sure it's good enough?" I ask standing up, with a little struggle.

"Yes, it's just our family. You don't need to dress for some award show." He rolls his eyes as I take the clothes. He grabs his long sleeve dark red button up, and puts in on. The whole time I watch him, and how his muscles flex as he does so. He meets my eyes smirking making me snap my head to look away, probably turn a tomato red. "Like the show?"

"Stop." I drag out. Alex chuckles lifting my chin for my eyes to meet his.

"It's not like you haven seen me naked before." My eyes widen from his words making him laugh before placing a kiss to my lips. "Now get ready, and I'll be helping downstairs." He tells me walking away, and buttoning the last of the buttons on his shirt as he walks. I sigh looking back to my clothes before putting them on. Once my clothes are on, and look the way I want, I head to the bathroom to brush my hair out. It dried in tangles making me groan in pain as I yank the brush through.

Alex assured me his mom is fine, which is comforting. I can't wait to see her, and Justin. I'm just afraid to see Matt and his wife Jordan, and their kids. They don't live as close as the rest and haven't seen us since the pregnancy. I walk out of my room, and down the stairs hearing voices get louder. I stop at the bottom of the stairs listening to see who is here, and I take a deep breath knowing Matt and Jordan are all ready here. Before I can walk in Alex walks out. He stops his eyes meeting mine, and a small smile plays on his lips.

"Took you long enough, now time to greet your guests." He walks to me taking my hand. He kisses my lips quick before leading the way to the living room. All I can do is take a big breath before we are in the room. The talking stops as they all turn to see who is there. Matt first has a grin on his face as he comes my way, but as he comes closer he glances to my baby belly.

"Bianca? Why didn't you say anything?" Matt asks as he pulls me into a hug. I hug him back cautiously.

"I was afraid. School is already hell." I whisper the last part as he pulls back. His eyes narrow at my words before he glances to Alex.

"What are people saying at school?"

"How about we talk later." Alex whispers. Matt nods his head before moving aside for Jordan to see me. Jordan hugs me tightly happy to see me. I blink not realizing she even came into this room.

"Congratulations, we missed you." She says pulling back.

"Thank you, and I missed you guys too."

"Where are the cousins?" Alex asks. Jordan chuckles looking behind her.

"Somewhere with Tony and Kait. Maddie is helping with food, though. How have you two been?" She asks, more interested in what we have to say than where the kids ran off to.

"Apart from the fact that I have a baby growing in me- good. Stressful, but good." Jordan nods her head understanding. She glances to Alex before looking back to me.

"And just so we are clear, Alex is the father?" She raises an eyebrow at me. My eyes widen as I look between Matt and Jordan.

"Aunt Jordan, don't do that to her. Yes, I'm the father." Alex says groaning the first sentence. To my surprise she grinds wider than she was before. She then squeals looking to Matt, who raises an eyebrow at her.

"I have to go find Jade and Nicole." She squeals out before taking off towards the kitchen. Matt looks to Alex gripping his shoulder tightly.

"Congrats you two. Alex you break her heart and leave her I'll kick your ass." Then Matt looks to me, still gripping Alex's shoulder. "Bianca, if you leave Alex with the baby not wanting it, and break his heart I will kick your ass. Understand?" He asks eyeing both of us.

"Yes." We respond at the same time. A grin breaks out in Matt's lips happy with our response.

"Great, now lets get this Christmas party on!" He cheers. I laugh as Alex wraps his arms around me once Matt walks after his wife. I look up to him smiling.

"That went well."

"Indeed it did," he kisses my head, "my mom's cousins are coming tomorrow, though, with their families. That should be fun." I feel my eyes widen as I turn in his hold to face him.

"Are they really? Shit. Alex, they are going to look at us differently." Alex shakes his head moving his arms so his hands cup my face. I look into blue his eyes, and take a deep breath.

"Bee, if Matt and Jordan were fine with it they won't be a problem." He assures.

"Aye love birds, food." Austin walks towards us. Alex lets me go, reluctantly, so I can greet Austin in a hug.

"Hello to you too." I laugh. Austin hugs me as tight as the baby will allow before letting me free.

"How is my little niece or nephew?" He asks a grin on his face. I see Holly come up to stand next to him giving Alex and I a warm smile. I smile back as Austin wraps his arm around her. I look down to my baby belly, and rest my right hand on it, rubbing small circles.

"Really good actually. I felt the baby kick last night." I smile thanking about my little baby.

"Wait! Why didn't you wake me?" Alex exclaims. I shrug giving him a small smile before looking back to a chuckling Austin. Holly just smiles widely at both of us making me grin back.

"Okay, time for food." I say, grabbing Alex's hand. I pull Alex along to the dining room for dinner, and I can feel Austin and Holly following us. This is going to be an eventful Christmas._________________________________

_____Hope you liked it

If you did please show it some love

Love you all

XO

Chapter twenty: Christmas part 2

"Just wake the damn kids already." A familiar male voice wakes me.

"No, they had a long night." I groan snuggling more into Alex's side.

"What were they doing? Fucking?"

"Jake! Don't talk like that." A familiar female voice scolds.

"They better shut up." Alex mutters in my ear. I groan in agreement feeling his arm tighten around my waist. I groan again feeling the baby kick me. "What's wrong?" I open my eyes to see his blue ones alert watching me.

"Baby is kicking again." I say, and as if on cue another kick is felt. I close my eyes, and feel Alex rest a hand on my stomach rubbing soothing circles. I feel him move his body down until his face is over my baby belly, which makes me cold.

"You have to stop kicking so hard, baby. Mommy is hurting, getting a boo boo. We can't be giving mommy a boo boo. Can you please stop your kicking for a little, for mommy and for daddy?" He whispers over the material of his tee shirt I wore to bed. He moves to now hover over me, his face just above mine. He lowers his head so his lips just whisper over mine. I can see the stubble that covers his face from two days of not shaving making my mouth water.

"Better?" He whispers. All I can do is nod my head as I lick my lips. Alex lets out a sound that seems to be a mix between a groan and a grunt. Before I know it his lips are claiming mine, and I let him with a moan. I wrap my arms around his neck, and my hands find their way into his hair.

"We can't." I pant as I break away for air. He kisses along my jaw, and down my neck.

"Why not? It won't hurt the baby." He says between kisses. I bite my lip to hold in a moan.

"That's not what I meant." My words come out breathless. A sudden knock on the door makes us jump, Alex swearing.

"Kids, we all want to open presents." I hear Nicole.

"Get your asses up, and take a cold shower." I hear Alex's one and only uncle Jake. My eyes widen as I meet Alex's, and his face is a light tint of pink. Alex smiles at me before leaning his head towards mine.

"Your cute when you blush." I groan pushing him away. "Start getting dressed. I have to go take a cold shower." He whispers before sprinting to the bathroom.

--

"So, the cold shower was needed?" Matt raises an eyebrow. I look to see Alex's cheeks tint pink. Alex keeps his eyes on the ground, and moves his arm to not be around me anymore.

"Um,"

"Matt, don't harass them." Nicole rolls her eyes. Matt just smirks to the other dads in the room.

"Wow, how old are all of you men?" My mom asks shaking her head.

"Physically or mentally?" Vlad asks.

"Ugh, hopeless." Veronica groans. All the mom's share a look agreeing.

"Mommy, look what I got." Our eyes all go to the little kids. We all sit watching the youngest kids, which are three, five, eight, and ten years old, play with their new toys. I smile leaning into Alex's side, and he wraps his arm around me, letting out a sigh I rub my belly as the baby kicks some more. I look around to see everyone talking and smiling, I watch my mom a little longer. She is watching everything, but she seems pale. She quickly jumps up, and runs to the bathroom down here, and I watch my dad run after her. We all look at each other not knowing what the hell just happened.

"Hold up, you two are together now?" Vlad asks pulling everyone's attention. Alex and I smile at each other before looking to Vlad.

"Yup." Alex kisses my head.

"Was this before or after you knocked her up?" Jamie smacks the back of Dan's head from his words. "I mean after she got pregnant." He fixes.

"Before." I sigh.

"Was it like a drunken thing like with Nicole and Justin?" Jake asks.

"Hey!" Alex's parents shout together. Jake only shrugs making his wife, Veronica, shake her head.

"I swear you never grow up. Little Ryder over here acts older sometimes, and he is five." She sighs. Jake gasps at her words looking to their youngest playing.

"Well, Blake acts older than you." He states. I roll my eyes at them. Blake is ten, and is just on his 3DS playing a new game he just got. Blake looks more like Jake, but with his mom's eyes, while Ryder looks more like his mom, but has Jake's eyes. Maya, the three year old, starts crying trying to reach up to her daddy. Dan picks her up, and holds her close rocking her in his arms. Sofia, Mays's twin, crawls on the ground trying to get to her brother, who is texting on his new phone by the tree. He is Trevor and is fourteen, and he looks like a mini Dan while his sisters are a perfect mix of both parents.

Matt is trying to take the phone his daughter, Maddie, just upgraded to away. She is a year older than Alex and I, but she acts like she is still thirteen. Then there is Lucas, who is with Jordan whining over getting the wrong Nike sneakers. He is an annoying thirteen year old, who bonds really well with my siblings. Lucas looks like a mini Matt, which is scary, and Maddie looks like neither of them, all she has are Jordan's eyes. Vlad and Francesca have triplets, bless their soul, Ella, Jayden, and Omar. Their triplets all just turned 16, and have those three they didn't want more kids. Ella looks just like her mom while the boys look nothing like their parents.

"Stop it you two." Vlad groans.

"When is breakfast?" I whisper to Alex. He smiles at me holding in a laugh. Everyone starts laughing too making me hide my face in Alex's shoulder.

"That's cute." Matt grins. "I'm going to go check on my sister, you guys can start getting the food ready." He says standing up.

"Good. I am starving."

"Well, you are eating for two." Jamie smiles at me.

"Hold on, where are my parents?" Justin questions as he stands up.

"They went to visit your sister this year." Nicole tells him. He frowns nodding his head before walking to the kitchen.

"Mommy I'm hungry." Ryder tells Veronica as he pulls her hair.

"I know, baby. Lets go help get it ready." She says standing up. I watch Jake watch her walk away, and the love in his eyes makes me smile.

"Can we go do something fun?" Omar asks.

"We should eat first though." Jayden tosses a small ball above his head, and catches it.

"I think I'm dying of boredom." Ella says dramatically putting a hand on her forehead, falling to the ground.

"Stop being a drama queen." Lucas mutters.

"Heard that." She sneers. I look to Alex annoyance written on my face.

"We might only have one." He frowns at that.

"I could always persuade you." I raise an eyebrow making him smirk. He leans towards me and places a kiss on my neck making me shudder.

"What are you doing?" Blake asks.

"Yeah, what are you doing?" Jake asks with a stern look.

"Persuading." Alex shrugs. I groan hiding my face in Alex's shoulder agai n.______________________________________Hope you liked it

Let my know what you think

Love you all

XO

Chapter twenty one: test owner found

I snuggle into Alex's side more as he takes his after school nap. His arm is wrapped around me tightly, keeping me close. I sigh opening my eyes only to blink from the bright light. I glance up to see he is still out, which brings a grin to my face. All I have wanted to do since he came cover was jump him, these hormones are making me crazy. I gently trace patterns on his chest before I trail my fingers down it. I take my other hand and trace his facial features.

I smile kissing his chest lightly before his neck, and his cheek. I kiss the corner of his mouth making him stir slightly. My hand reaches the rim of his boxers making his body move a little. Growing annoyed I wrap my leg around his waist purposely rubbing it against his friend making him jump. Alex's eyes snap open meeting mine, and before I can process anything his lips are on mine. My eyes flutter closed as a moan escapes my mouth as he hungrily kisses me. Alex moves us, rolling, so he hovers over me.

"What was that for?" He asks between placing kisses on my neck.

"I blame the hormones." I whisper. Alex chuckles against my skin before looking into my eyes.

"That's the only reason?" He raises an eyebrow.

"No." I breathe out. Alex smirks before his lips claim mine. I kiss him back wanting him, no needing him.

"Good, but babe my parents are home." He warns me, yet his voice is strained. I frown at him wanting all of him right now.

"I'll be quiet." I whisper kissing the corner of his lips. He groans before he devours my lips making my core burn, and a low moan erupt from me.

--

I frown at Alex as he packs his clothes. He got called for another photo shoot thing in Australia, and I can't go. Everyone freaked out when I said I wanted to go with Alex, after he finally told them about his job. Austin kept making jokes about it, but Alex ignored it. "Do you have to go?" He stops stuffing clothes in a suitcase, and looks up to me.

"Bee, don't make this that much harder. I'll only be gone a week." He leans over placing a kiss on my cheek.

"What am I suppose to do for a week?" I pout. Alex chuckles shaking his head. He turns around heading to the attached bathroom.

"Hey Bee," Alex walks back out with his bathroom things. "When I get back we are moving into the apartment."

"Really? It is a bachelor pad, not anything for a small family." He gives me a pointed look.

"Babe, I haven't been there since our night there. I barely ever went there in the first place, so how could I have made it a bachelor pad?" I sigh getting up off the bed, a hand on my stomach. "Plus we just have to make it for us, and that won't be hard."

"Whatever. I hate this." I pout rubbing my belly. Alex moves to stand in front of me resting both hands on my belly.

"Whats wrong?" His voice is filled with concern.

"Not knowing what our baby is." Alex chuckles.

"We can always find out in the next appointment, but only if you want." I bite my lips at his words. I look into his blue eyes seeing confusion. "What's wrong?"

"Won't that ruin the surprise of it?"

"Babe, it won't ruin anything. If you want to wait we will wait." Alex assures me. "Ugh, babe I got to finish packing." He groans before kissing my lips quick. He walks away back to where he is packing. I sigh before walking out of the room heading downstairs. I walk right into the kitchen seeing Justin and Nicole looking at something in Justin's hands. I peek over Nicole's shoulder seeing an ultrasound picture. I smile seeing they are still looking at it excitedly, even though it was from when I was only a few months. The first picture.

"Why are you looking at that one?" I ask. They both jump looking to me with wide eyes, and Justin tries to hide it behind him.

"Bianca," Nicole starts. My eyebrows furrow before I take a step back, everything seems to click.

"Wait, you're...?" I can't find the words to say it.

"Yes, I'm pregnant. I'm not trying to take your spotlight either, I'm sorry." I shake my head.

"I'm not upset or mad. You should be happy, excited." I hug her, and she hugs me back sniffling.

"We are. Bianca, you can't tell our kids yet. We are telling them tonight at dinner." She whispers in my ear. I nod my head pulling back smiling to her.

"So, it was your test at my house?" Confusion covers her face making my eyes widen. "It wasn't yours?"

"Is it your mom's?"

"Shit, I didn't think to ask. Maybe that's what's up with her." I hurry out of Alex's house before walking into mine. I stop taking a breath holding my stomach. My mom stops in the hallway watching me cautiously, she holds a laundry basket in her arms.

"What's wrong, hun?" She puts the basket down walking over to me. I take a deep breath before looking into her eyes. I can see them studying me trying to read me.

"Be honest with me, okay?"

"Of course."

"Are you pregnant?" She freezes in her spot, her eyes widening. "If you are I'm not mad, shocked but not mad." I try to assure her, wanting her to know she can tell me. She opens her mouth before she closes it.

"I was." I frown at her words as tears turn her eyes to glass. I hug her feeling my eyes start to water along with hers.

"I'm sorry mom."

"Don't be baby, if it was meant to happen it would have." She squeezes me in her arms.____Hope you liked it. Sorry for the late update... this chapter is not my best. Writers block is a bitch and this is what became of it.

If you did like it please show it some love.

Love you all

XO

Chapter twenty two: new home

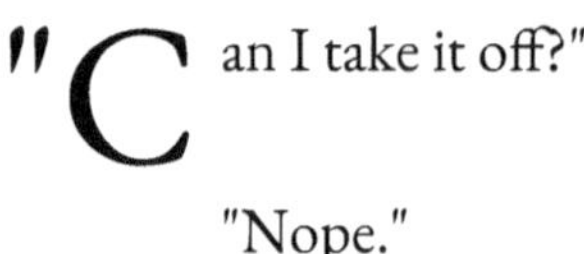

"**C**an I take it off?"

"Nope."

"Why not?"

"I've told you more than once."

"But Austin." I whine.

"Ugh, stop whining. My brother might deal with that but I don't."

"You cave when I whine." Holly buts in. I laugh knowing Austin is rolling his eyes right now.

"Why can't you tell me where you are taking me?"

"It's a surprise."

"You see I get that, but this pregnant lady over here would like to know where you are blindly taking her." I hear Holly laugh making me smile.

"I swear if you are taking me to a surprise baby shower I'm out."

"Damnit."

"Ha! I knew it."

"I was being sarcastic." Austin states dryly. I roll my hidden eyes. "Plus it's a little too early for one, don't you think?"

"I think seven months is a good time." I point out.

"Probably more towards the end of month seven." Holly muses.

"True true." I agree.

"Anyway, Alex wants us to do this."

"Oh my God, he wants you to kill me. I swear I'm going to haunt his ass and kill him myself."

"Damn girl, calm down."

"Austin," Holly scolds. "You never tell a woman to calm down."

"Shit, your right. Sorry Bianca."

"Apology not accepted." I cross my arms over my chest, and hear Holly try to hold in a laugh.

"Are you kidding."

"No, no I am not." I hear Austin groan making me bite back a grin. "There is one way I will accept it."

"I'm not taking the blindfold off."

"Darn it."

"Just a little longer." Holly assures. "So, are you two keeping the gender a secret or did you not find out?"

"Alex and I are waiting for this little bean to be born."

"Awe that's cute. What do you want it to be?"

"Honestly I don't care. I just want my baby to be healthy."

"Well, I want it to be a boy." Austin says.

"I don't remember anyone asking you." I say Turing my head towards his voice.

"I'm hoping for you to have a girl." Holly says.

"That would be cute. Our little princess." I smile.

"Am I the only one who can't have an opinion?" Austin whines.

"Basically." Holly and I say at the same time.

--

After the dragging car ride of being blindfolded Austin finally parked the car. I wait for Austin, and Holly, to get out to open the door for me. I feel the cool air rush over my body making me shiver. I feel a presence come closer reaching behind me for the blindfold. By the smell of his cologne I know it is Austin. As soon as the blindfold is off my eyes blink from the blinding light. As I adjust to the world I notice we are at Alex's apartment complex.

"Um why blindfold me? I've been here already." I look between the two.

"Wait, you have?" Austin asks with wide eyes. I nod my head thinking back to that night. That has to be the night our little bean was conceived. "Oh god your cheeks are bright red. Please tell me you two did not fuck."

"Can we go in?"

"Oh god you two actually fucked in there." Austin groans walking away. Holly laughs shaking her head as she looks towards Austin before looking back to me.

"That must have been the night, huh?" I bite my lip giving a small nod.

"I didn't want to hear that!" Austin whines.

"What's going on over here?" I hear Olivia's voice. I snap my head to where it came from, my lips forming a grin seeing her walk over.

"Hey girly." She grins. She gives me her hands to help me out of the car. As soon as I'm out I hug her tight, but not too tight to hurt my baby.

"I've missed you."

"I missed you too, Bianca." We pull back as we feel Austin come closer. "Wow, baby grew from last time."

"Come on, Alex wants to know what we should do for paint colors, and decorating for your new place." Austin smiles. I nod my head, and we all walk up towards the apartment. Luckily it is on the second flour, so I don't have to travel too much. My seven month belly holds my baby, who is getting heavier, making everything harder. I get tired easily, especially from going up a lot of stairs. I caress my baby belly as I follow the group up the stairs.

We get to the door and Austin wastes no time in opening it. He unlocks the door before pushing it open. He turns back to me smiling. "Soon to be mommy first." I smile before walking pass him into the dark apartment. I hit the light switch, and gasp at the sight. My hands come up covering my mouth as my eyes water looking to Alex. He has a grin on his face opening his arms up, as if gesturing towards the room. I look around seeing how much work was put into it.

They repainted the room, and brought in new furniture matching to my style. I feel the tears run down my face as this apartment starts to feel like home. I can see pictures of us all in frames on the walls, and coffee table. I walk right into Alex's arms tears uncontrollably leaving my eyes running down my face.

"Do you like it, Bee?"

"I love it! Can I see the rest?"

"Of course, but first turn around." I turn around wiping my eyes seeing Austin, Olivia, and Holly at the entrance. They hold a banner saying welcome home. I smile turning back around to see Alex on the ground holding a small box. My hands fly to my mouth as a gasp leaves my mouth.

"Before you freak out, I'm not proposing- yet. My father did this, and I feel like it is right. Bianca, I promise to always love you, and our little bean. I promise to never leave you or let you go. I will fight for you, and to keep you no matter what. I will prove to you every day how much you mean to me, how much I love you.

"I give you this promise ring, to always remind you of my vow to you." My vision turns blurry as he takes my hand placing the ring on my finger. He stands up, and I wrap my arms around him, meeting our lips. I hear confetti go off from the three by the door, along with their cheers. Alex holds me as close as he can, his lips kissing me hungrily. I feel one hand leave my body before the door closes, and the hand returns.

"I love you." I whisper on his lips.

"I love you, Bee."

"Make love to me." I feel his grip tighten as a low groan comes from his throat.

"Oh I will. Lets break in our new home." I squeal as he lifts me up by grabbing my thighs, and lifting me. ____Hope you liked it. That is their apartment layout up top of on the side.

What do you want the baby to be, boy or girl?

Love you all

XO

Chapter twenty three: new thoughts to cloud my mind

I walk into the kitchen wanting some chocolate with whipped cream on it. I frown only seeing the chocolate, but take it anyway. Taking a bite of the chocolatey goodness a moan escapes as my eyes flutter close. Arms wrap around me making my eyes snap open, but I melt into their embrace. "Damn, Bee." He whispers in my ear.

Taking another bite I do the same thing, and I can feel his friend coming to life. I feel his body tense a little bit as his hold tightens. "Fuck, babe." He groans as he grinds his hips against my ass.

"Someone is happy." I muse. He groans in response kissing my jaw. He kisses my neck sucking on the skin.

"I want you so bad right now." His voice is full of lust. I smile turning around to face him. Making his friend rub against my skin before my front. He groans grinding his hips a little more.

"Then take me." I kiss his lips making him moan, which seems to turn to a growl. A knock on the door makes us jump. I frown moving away from his addicting body. He looks to me with wide eyes before running to take a cold shower. I shake my head laughing a little before opening the door. Chris and Nini tackle me in a hug, for the most part. I laugh hugging them back.

"I missed you girly."

"Love you girl, but where is my bro?" I shake my head at Chris's words.

"Shower. Anyway, make yourselves at home." I move out of the way letting them in before shutting the door.

"Cute place you two got." I smile sitting on the couch. I hold my belly as I slowly lower myself down.

"Thank you."

"So, got any names for my little niece or nephew?" Chris asks.

"We got a few in mind, but they are a secret until our bean is born." They both groan not liking that answer.

"Not fair."

"Yeah, you can't tell your best friends?"

"Nope. Not even our family knows."

"So, what is the plan today?"

"Whatever you guys want to do." Alex says walking into the room. He has a towel around his shoulder and basketball shorts on, his underwear showing at the top. I look away before I get all hot and bothered more than before left me.

--

"So, how is this online schooling going?" I sigh looking to my mom. She slides a sandwich over towards me as she takes a seat next to me at the table.

"I guess it's good. I go on every time Alex goes to school. Otherwise he would be too much of a distraction." I smile grabbing the sandwich.

"I see," she chuckles, "this is a nice place you go here." I finally got her to come over to Alex and I's place. She wasn't keen on my staying here, but knows it's best for the baby to live with both parents.

"Thank you." I grin with a mouthful of my delicious food.

"When does soccer start?" I frown shrugging my shoulders.

"Alex hasn't said yet. All I know is he has scouts still talking to him about basketball." She nods her head taking a bite of her own sandwich. I close the laptop finishing the last math question.

"What do you two plan to do after high school, when the baby is here." I rest my right hand on my belly looking down to it. With only about three months to go everything is becoming more real.

"We haven't talked about it. I haven't even thought about it."

"Well, it's something you should be thinking of. No matter what you choose I'll be here to support you, and so will your father."

"Thanks mom." She smiles at me just as the door bangs open. We both look to see Alex dragging himself through the door. He stops dead in his tracks as his eyes go from my mom to myself.

"Sorry, long day." My mom chuckles shaking her head. Alex comes up to me and hugs me kissing my cheek. "How are you?"

"I'm fine, baby is fine." He smiles at that before looking to my mom.

"How are you?"

"Wonderful. How is your mom doing? I haven't gotten the chance to talk to her yet today." I smile at that before taking another big bite of my sandwich.

"She is doing good. I still can't believe I'm going to be a big brother, and a father."

"I'm guessing your father's pull out game is weaker than it used to be." She sighs. Alex chokes on air as my eyes widen. My head snaps so my eyes glare at my mom. "What? Did I say something?"

"Mom! Why did you just say that?"

"What girls talk." I gag hearing that. Even though I know how true that statement is. "Change of topic: did you get the save the date?"

"Um I don't know? For Austin and Holly?"

"Yes. They sent them out beginning of the week."

"I'll go get the mail and see." Alex says, and he leaves to go see. I narrow my eyes on my mom.

"I can't believe you."

"Hey, I'm the mom. It's my job."

"Make that weird mom."

"I knew you would get it." I roll my eyes at her groaning. "Anyway, your siblings want me to tell you they have the baby names picked out."

"Oh no, really?"

"Yeah, and I'm just going to say they aren't the best. And I do not want my grandchild to be named with any they picked."

"What were some of them?"

"I'm not going to even go there. They love to use their imagination though." I cringe at the thought. "Exactly."

"Got it!" Alex cheers holding the envelope in the air as he walks in. He throws the rest of the mail on the table before hanging the save the date on the fridge. "May 30th." Alex grins.

"Of next year?"

"Yup." My mom gushes. "Oh I love weddings."

"Easy mom." She frowns at me crossing her arms playfully.

"Wow, my brother is getting married." Alex mutters to himself as he lowers himself into the seat next to me.

"Awe little Austin is growing up." I coo.

"Damn I'm getting old." My mom mumbles under her breath. "What has the world become?" Alex and I look to her our eyebrows furrowed. She looks to us with wide eyes.

"Um?"

"Shit, was that out loud?" All we can do is nod our heads.____________
____________________Hope you liked it. Sorry for the long wait, and not so good chapter. It's been crazy, so I apologize.

If you did like it please show some love, it will get better and faster updates. This was more of a filler.

Love you all

XO

Chapter twenth four: i did not want this

"N"ope."

"Yes you are."

"No, I'm not going."

"You don't even know where we are going." I shoot her a look making her stop for a second.

"Why the hell would you tell me to dress up more then?" I shoot back. She groans grabbing at her hair and pulling.

"Bianca, just go out with me. Like old times."

"Nini, I'd love to, but I know this is a set up."

"For what exactly?"

"A baby shower." She rolls her eyes at me. She falls back onto my bed just done.

"Just come on. Don't make me call Olivia." She threatens. I narrow my eyes on her as she sits up.

"You wouldn't." She holds her phone unlocked in her hand.

"Oh I would, so don't test me." My eyes narrow on her even more as I cross my arms over my chest.

"Call her, I'm not going. I look like a fat cow." I whine.

"You leave me no choice." Nini frowns as she presses Olivia's number. My eyes widen at her knowing Olivia won't have my whining.

"Nini!"

"Hello, Olivia." Nini smiles bringing the phone to her ear. "She won't." I groan walking into the connecting bathroom, and shut the door.

--

Olivia, gently, pulls me out of the car. I look at the restaurant in front of us groaning. I cross my arms over my chest. I don't know why they want to make this a big deal. I didn't want to seem needy for baby things. I already started looking for things I need, and getting some.

"Stop. Bianca, this is something every first time mother has, so suck it up." I take a deep breath looking to Olivia. I feel Nini come stand next to me. I know I am probably overreacting to all of this, but I blame the pregnancy hormones.

"Okay, lets go." We walk in, and walk right into a separate room filled with all of my close family. They all look over grinning, and I smile in return. I look around to see blue and pink decorations on tables, the walls, and even hanging from the ceiling. I look to Nini before looking to Olivia.

"You guys did all this?" I feel the tears in my eyes, and suddenly arms wrap around me.

"Do you like it, Queen?" I look up towards Alex's face smiling as a tear slips down my cheek.

"I love it." He turns me towards him frowning. He looks into my eyes concern swimming in them. He cups my face in his hands as he looks right into my eyes.

"Then why are you crying?" He wipes a tear with his thumb.

"They're happy tears." I lean forward letting my lips meet his.

"Aye can you not do that here?" I hear uncle Jake call. I pull away from Alex smiling as some tears still trickle down.

"Come on people, place your guess. Boy or girl?" I turn around to see a table with a box with boy or girl written on it. Little papers are next to it for people to put their guess on.

"Do the winners get a prize?" I whisper to Olivia.

"Just the satisfaction of guessing right."

"They should get something." I frown. She rolls her eyes at me before she heads off to some guy I've only seen once before. I look to Nini, who is now in Chris' embrace.

"And what would you give them?" She asks.

"Good question." I take Alex's hand and walk towards the center of the room, where the majority or the people are. On the way I see a table covered in gifts. I stop looking at it.

"Just except it, Bee. They were going to bring our baby something." I nod my head letting out a breath.

"I know, but I honestly don't know what or how to feel about it." I whisper to him. He nods his head in understanding.

"Bianca darling." My Mom grins coming up to me. I smile seeing her, and Alex's Mom right beside her. His mom is showing off small little baby bump.

"We were worried you wouldn't show."

"Well, here I am. I couldn't not come, and you know as well as I do Olivia would have dragged me in by my ear." They chuckle nodding their heads.

"That's true, she was always spirited."

"I didn't know her boyfriend was going to be here." I say looking towards the two of them.

"You and me both." I look back to Nicole.

"Mom, she did say she has a good feeling about where they are going." Alex sighs wrapping his arm around me.

"There is the mom to be." I look over to see my grandparents, from my mom's side. They hurry over to me wrapping me in a hug, which Alex made a little awkward. He kept his arm around me the whole time.

"I didn't know you guys were going to be here." I smile at them resting a hand on my baby belly.

"Why wouldn't we?" My grandmother looks a little hurt making me frown.

"Of course we had to come see our little granddaughter who is expecting a baby." My grandfather smiles.

"Thank you for coming." Alex smiles to them, which gains their attention.

"Take care of them, boy." My grandfather tells him giving Alex a good stare down.

"Will do sir." Alex says with the most amount of confidence he has in him.

"Now, come on let's go find our other grandkids." My grandmother says. I laugh looking around to see if I spot my siblings, which I don't.

"If you find them tell them I say hi, and to find me." They smile giving me one more hug before leaving.

"I need to sit down." I state before walking to a table, and taking a seat. Alex follows my lead sitting down next to me. I look out to see everyone mingling and having a good time, which is what brings a smile to my lips.

"Someone seems happy." I look to Alex kissing his cheek.

"Everyone is happy too, it is making me happy. Thank you for getting this to happen." He kisses my cheek wrapping his arms around me.

"You're welcome, but mostly thank my sister and Nini. They only came to me when they were stumped." I sigh leaning against him. Everything is going perfectly right now, and I can't ask for more. It only worries me that something bad is going to happen and break all of this good.___________
_________________________Hope you liked it.

If you did please show some love

What do you want boy or girl?

Love you all

XO

Chapter twenty five: shopping

I walk into the store holding the shopping list in my hand. My other hand holds my pregnant belly. I grab a cart pushing it to where I need to go. I stop looking at the fruits trying to see which ones are good. I stop hearing a voice I didn't want to.

"Bianca, is that you?" I freeze hearing AJ's voice. I take a deep breath before I turn around. His eyes widen as he gives me a once over.

"Hi."

"Wow, you changed." I frown at his words. His staring makes me shift my body trying to get in a comfortable position.

"Thanks." I sigh sarcastically. His eyes go to mine, and I can see the slightest bit of regret.

"How are you doing?" I blink my eyes shocked by his question. "I see a Alex in school all the time, and he seems miserable without you."

"I'm fine. Online schooling when Alex is at school, and then we do stuff together."

"Sure, why isn't he here then?"

"He is at some meeting for his big project he is working on."

"Right. I'm guessing that's why he was hanging out with Claire." My body stiffens hearing that information. I feel my heart clench aching in my chest.

"He wouldn't." I shake my head. AJ raises an eyebrow cocking his head to the side.

"Why would he want to ruin his chance at a full ride soccer scholarship? With you and the baby he has no chance."

"He didn't s-"

"He didn't tell you? Oops, guess you know now. He wants to turn it down because he knows he has to stay for you." I crumple the list in my hand. We haven't talked about the future yet, but why wouldn't he tell me?

"It was nice talking to you again, oh wait what is it?"

"We aren't finding out until the baby is born." I tell him automatically.

"Well, whatever it is I hope it doesn't end up like you." With that he walks away leaving me stunned. Tears sting my eyes as I stare at the spot he just stood. I take out my phone just needing to hear his calming voice. After the third ring he picks up.

"Bee, is something wrong?"

"I-" words don't come out as my throats becomes thick. Tears start to fall from my eyes, and I can hear him swear under his breath.

"Where are you?"

"Grocery store." I force out.

"Okay, I'm coming. The meeting ended as soon as you called. I'm going to stay on the phone too okay?"

"Okay." I cry.

"Do you need to go to the hospital?"

"No." He lets out a breath a little relieved that our baby is okay.

"Okay, I'm in the car. Just listen to my voice, babe." He tells me. I nod my head forgetting he can't see me. "Bee?"

"Yes?"

"Just making sure you are still there." I sniffle in response. "Did you see someone from school?" At his question I start to sob. He curses, and I can hear his car accelerate. "I'm five minutes away. Did you do the shopping yet?"

"No." I whisper through tears.

"Okay, where is your mom? Wasn't she bringing you?"

"She said she had to go somewhere and will be back to pick me up when I'm done." I force every word out through the lump in my throat.

"Okay, I'm pulling in. I'll park and then help you shop." I watch looking through the window that is not too far away, and see his black Nissan. I look around seeing some people giving me weird looks. "Found a spot."

"Honey are you okay?" I look to see a young mother holding her child, who seems to be only a year old. I nod my head, which only makes her frown. "Take a few deep breathes for me." She instructs.

"I'm walking into the store, where are you?" I hear Alex's voice. Taking a deep breath like she said I answer Alex. He is quick to find me hanging up the phone call. His arms wrap around me bringing me to his chest. I breath in his comforting scent, and relax at the safety his presence brings.

"I'm guessing your the boyfriend, and father." The young mom says. I move my head to look to here, and smile at her. She smiles seeing me calmer.

"Yes, did you see who made her so upset by any chance?" Alex asks. I can just imagine how mad he is on the inside. She thinks about it.

"Yeah. It was some guy around your age. He seemed athletic dark hair, and wore a baseball shirt."

"Thank you, and what is your name by the way? I'm Alex and this is Bianca." She smiles shifting her baby slightly in her arms.

"I'm Marisa, and this is James." I smile at the little boy before looking to her.

"Well thank you Marisa. Thank you for stopping to try and help calm Bee down."

"No problem, I've gone through moments like that too. What are you having?"

"It's a surprise." Alex says, his voice giving away his grin. She grins at that.

"So was James. The wait was annoying, but my husband and I both agreed. Congratulations by the way."

"Thank you." I pipe up. She smiles at me.

"You're very welcome. Well, I should get my shopping done, and I'm guessing you have to as well. Bye." She waves before walking along. I look up to Alex, who captures my lips with his right away. He pulls back only to pepper my face with kisses.

"Alex." I whine a smile automatically forming. He grins down at me.

"There is that beautiful smile." He kisses my lips quick.

"It was AJ." He tenses taking in a deep breath.

"Lets forget about it for now, and shop. We will talk about it after, okay?"

"Okay. I'll text my mom and tell her you are here, and will take me home." He smiles taking the list from my hand, and smooths it out. We start walking as I text my mom, and I follow his lead to where we are going. I smile taking one of his hands happy he is here.

"Thank you."

"For what?" I feel him look down towards me making me look up to him.

"Coming."

"Bee, I'll always come."

"Really?" He stops walking looking at me as his eyebrows furrow.

"Why wouldn't I?"

"Never mind." I say looking down.

"Bianca," he lifts my chin up sunny eyes meet his. "is it was AJ said?" I nod my head butting my lip. Alex frowns kissing my forehead. "We will talk later, right now which cereal are we getting?" I laugh at him tapping his nose.

"The only one you eat." He grins at me.___________________________
____

Chapter twenty six: oh Chris

"So, we need to talk." I state. Alex looks at me mid bite before putting his sandwich down. He takes a deep breath running a hand through his damp hair. He just came home from practice and showered as I made sandwiches for dinner.

"Before you start I just want to say I was going to tell you." He tries to clear up. My eyebrows furrow as I stare at him.

"What are you talking about?"

"What are you talking about?" He questions back.

"I wanted to talk about our future. What the hell are you talking about?" His eyes widen before he clears his throat looking to his food.

"Nothing."

"Alex, look at me." My voice is stern making him look up to me. He gives me an innocent child look making my eyes narrow on him. "What did you do?" He lets out a breath running a hand through his damp hair again.

"I got a tattoo. It was supposed to be a surprise, but I guess the cat is out of the bag." My jaw drops as my eyes widen.

"What! When?" He looks over his shoulder mumbling something. "Alex." I say as if I am talking to a child who is in trouble. He looks back to me gulping.

"Two days ago."

"Who went with you?"

"Chris."

"I'm going to have a word with that boy." I mumble.

"You don't like tattoos?" I give Alex a pointed look.

"You know me better than anyone. Tattoos are a turn on."

"Then why are you upset?"

"I wanted to go with you." I frown. Alex gets up and kneels down in front of me. He cups my face in his hands. I look into his deep blue eyes, and my frown instantly goes away.

"It was a surprise though." He kisses my lips quick making a smile grace my lips. "Now, let's talk about what you wanted to."

"But I want to see the tattoo." Alex rolls his eyes at me a smile on his face.

"You can see it later." He winks at me. "Damn I love when you blush." I look away knowing I probably turned redder even though I can't really tell. I clear my throat looking back to Alex.

"You can take your seat. We have to talk about something important." He takes his seat taking a bite of his food.

"I know, I know, the future." He says through a mouth full of food. I roll my eyes at him shaking my head.

"Is it true that you can get a full ride?" He stops chewing. "So it is."

"Where did you hear that?"

"AJ." I force his name out. Alex visibly tenses up at the mention of his name. I watch his blue eyes darken as his jaw clenches.

"That fucker."

"Alex. Why didn't you tell me?"

"I can't take it."

"Why not?"

"You are going to need me when the baby is born." His eyes stare right into mine showing me his emotions.

"Alex, if you want to play and go to school we can work that in. I don't want you to put an end to what you truly want." I take his hand across the table.

"Maybe if it's a local college, and can work with us, I'll look into it." I smile at his response. "We will have to see what happens, and talk about it then."

"Okay."

"Now, what do you plan on doing?" I stare at him blankly.

"What?"

"We talked about an option for me, but what about you?"

"I'll be taking care of the baby." He raises an eyebrow at me.

"So, you can put a stop to what you want, but I can't?" I roll my eyes at him.

"Alex that's n-"

"Don't say what you are about to. Bianca, you are going to get an education and you are going to do what you want for school." I just blink at him as he cut me off. I let out a breath looking down to my half eaten sandwich.

"Honestly I don't know what I want. I always wanted to do art, but that's as far as I got." I look up to Alex meeting his sincere eyes.

"Look into it, Bee." Alex smiles at me. I smile back placing a hand on my belly.

"I will."

--

I cling onto Alex with my arms wrapped around his torso. My head rests right next to his tattoo on his upper right chest. I smile reading the words again. The words 'famiglia per sempre' written in thick straight letters. The famiglia is written largely on top of the per sempre. "Why did you choose Italian?"

"Well, my family is Italian. I thought it sounded nice, and looks like what I wanted."

"Did it hurt?"

"Not as much as I was expecting." I nod my head debating if I should trace it. It could still be sore. I feel his lips press a kiss to my head.

"Does it hurt now?" Alex chuckles holding me tighter.

"No, not really." I kiss the tattoo before looking up meeting his eyes. His lips are on mine instantly making me gasp surprised. My lips begin to move with his making him hold me tighter. I moan against his lips making him groan rolling us. He makes it so my back is on the mattress and he is hovering over him.

"Damn Bee, you are such a turn on." He groans against my lips. His start to kiss down my jaw before they suck on my neck.

"Alex." I breath out breathless.

"Say my name." He whispers on my skin as his hand slips into my pajama pants.

"Alex." I moan as I feel his fingers on my skin. I feel his lips smile against my skin making me shiver. A knocking on our door freezes us in our spot. We both look to each other then towards our door. Alex gets up looking to me our eyes meet, and I can see he wants me to stay quiet and stay here. I just nod my head letting him know I will. He gets up grabbing his baseball bat he keeps by the door.

I sit myself up on the bed hoping for it to not be anything bad. I let out a breath as I hear an all too familiar voice. "Why the hell do you have a bat?"

"Why the hell are you here so late?"

"What the fuck are you talking about? It's only nine."

"Sometimes I wonder where your brain is." I hear Alex coming towards the bedroom. He sticks his head in with an annoyed look on his face. "It just Chris." I roll my eyes as I try to get out of bed. Alex comes over and helps me up without saying anything.

"Why is he here right now? I'm tired." I pout. Alex shrugs leading the way to our friend. I smile at Chris, which is a little forced.

"Hey Bianca." Chris grins hugging me tight. I hug him back before he lets me go.

"So, what do we owe this unexpected visit to?" His face then falls making Alex and I share a look.

"I think I fucked up."

"How?"

"Some of the cheerleaders were trying to flirt with me, and kept touching me. They wouldn't listen when I said to stop, and now Nini won't talk to me." I sigh giving him another hug.

"I'll talk to her about it. How did you try and get out of that situation?"

"I tried walking away to get to Nini, but they wouldn't let me go."

"Damn those bitches."

"You said it man."____Hope you like it, sorry for the late update guys.

I've been having bad anxiety lately and that has been making it hard for me to write, but I am trying. So bare with me I'm sorry

If you liked it please leave a comment and vote,

Baby name ideas?

Love you all

XO

Chapter twenty seven: what about school?

- -

"Go Alex!" I shout along with his mom, Nicole. He kicks the ball into the goal, and the goalie misses the ball. Nicole grins looking at me as I do the same to her.

"Did you see my boy?" I laugh nodding my head. Justin next to her rolls his eyes as he hands a packet of twizlers to Nicole. Nini sighs next to me making me frown looking to her. She watches Chris jogging back to his starting position. I wrap an arm around her bringing her to my side.

"Nini, he tried to get out of their claws. He loves you, and can't see any other girl as he sees you." She looks up to me with glassy eyes.

"Really?"

"Can't you see he isn't really in the game? He is beating himself up over it." She frowns looking back over to Chris.

"That's true." She sighs looking to me. "You should have heard what they said after." I frown at that, knowing all too well. We look back to the game hearing the whistle, and see our team with the ball. I smile watching Alex get open for his teammate to pass it. Chris gets it instead before passing it to Alex. Alex gives it one hard kick sending it straight into the net.

"I'm so proud of my baby boy." I hear Nicole. I smile looking over to her. Her baby belly is noticeable, and there are a few parents who keep eyeing her. Justin rests his hand on it so naturally as they watch their son play. I place a hand on my stomach a smile on my face as I look back out to see my baby's father on the field.

"Aye! Alex's baby momma! You prepared for him to leave you sorry ass." I look to see Andy and his buddy laughing.

"If I were you I'd shut the hell up!" Justin responds. Andy rolls his eyes.

"And what are you going to do old man?" I can feel the anger radiating from Justin as he glares daggers at the two. Andy's buddy just laughs at what he came up with.

"Boy you don't know who the hell you are talking to. Just wait and keep an eye out, and hope none of my boys, or myself, finds you." With that said the two gulp turning around towards the game.

"Eww the sluts here." I hear a girl whisper, loudly, to her friend right behind us.

"You shouldn't say that about yourself hun. It's not nice." Nicole says turning to look to the girl. I hold in my laugh as I focus back to the game. I hear the girl gasp, and I can just picture the look on her face. She doesn't say anything though, so Nicole turns back to look at the game.

After the game ends we wait for Alex and Chris by the locker room. Justin wraps his arm around Nicole, and she leans into him smiling. I lean against the wall wanting Alex to hurry up and come out. Justin's phone rings making him groan as we all look to him. He takes it out frowning.

"Its work, I'll be right back." He walks away as he brings the phone to his ear.

"Ugh that restaurant." Nicole groans.

"I thought you liked it." She sighs looking at me.

"I do, but lately they have been calling constantly."

"It must be important then." I say offering a small smile. Alex and Chris come out all smiles on their faces. Nini gets tense next to me seeing Chris, but I know soon they will be all good after tonight.

--

I sigh brushing my hair trying to get the knots out. My stomach has been cramping up all day, which is not fun. Alex comes through the bathroom door with only a towel around his waist. He looks to me raising an eyebrow. "What's wrong?"

"The baby is just making things uncomfortable right now." I say rubbing my belly to try and ease the pain. Alex frowns coming over and wrapping his arms around me.

"I'm sorry, bee." He kisses my head before I feel his hand caress my belly. "Soon our little baby will be out." He kisses my lips quick.

"Wow, doesn't that scare you?" He looks into my eyes his lips playing a small smile.

"Of course I am, but the excitement overpowers it." I smile feeling the same way. "Hey, next game one of the scouts are coming." He tells me.

"Really? That's great!" I grin kissing his lips. He rolls his eyes before hugging me close.

"Just make sure our little angel doesn't decide to come out then." He whispers jokingly in my ear.

"Don't jinx it." I warn him. Alex just laughs before letting me go. He sighs before walking to his closet.

"Bee, are you really going to take a year off?" I look to him with raised eyebrows. He comes out looking to me as he pulls shorts on.

"Why wouldn't I?" He shrugs his shoulders coming to sit next to me.

"Is it what you want to do?"

"Alex, we talked about this." He sighs laying back on the bed. I look to him laying down too. He takes my hand in his bringing it to his lips to kiss.

"I know, I just feel bad."

"Don't feel bad. Alex, it's just the way things are going."

"Maybe I shouldn't try for the scholarship." I look at him like he lost it because clearly he did.

"Alex, you need this. Think about your future." He looks to me a small smile on his lips.

"I am." I smile shaking my head.

"Then you would know our baby needs you to have a good job. Which means you need schooling."

"That's not how my parents did it." He points out.

"Alex, we aren't your parents. Things have changed, it's been almost 18 years." He groans knowing I'm right. He kisses my forehead wrapping his arm around me. "Have Chris and Nini talked to each other?" I change the topic.

"I think that's what they are doing now." He sighs pulling me closer to him. I smile wrapping one arm around his torso.

"Good, they really needed to talk that over."

"For sure. If he had to stay here another night crying I'd lose it." I laugh in agreement.___________________________________Hope you liked it. Sorry for the long wait! College has taken a good chunk of time, but I'm figuring it out.

If you liked it please give this chapter some love

Love you all

XO

Chapter twenty eight: Alex?

I smile folding the blanket, and putting it in the crib for now. I look around the baby's room smiling to myself longing to hold my baby in my arms. I jump hearing the phone ring. I pick it up only for a smile to grace my lips. "Hi honey." My mom's voice rings.

"Hi Mom."

"Your father and I were wondering if you and Alex would want to come over for dinner."

"Of course. He's at school, but he'll agree. What time should we be over?"

"Seven. Oh and Alex's family will be here, his siblings are home for the weekend."

"Okay, we will be there." I grin into the phone. My mom chuckles finding my response amusing.

"See you later honey."

"Bye mom see you tonight." She hangs up, and so do I. I smile putting the phone back, and I walk into the kitchen hungry for something. I pout seeing nothing I want to eat. The door opens gaining my attention. I look towards it grinning as I see Alex trudging into the apartment. I frown seeing the stress that seems to take over his features.

"Alex?" He looks over to me a small smile gracing his lips.

"Hi babe." He shuts the door before kicking off his shoes. "I'm going to go shower off this practice stench." I nod my head as he walks off towards our bedroom. I frown following after him only to hear him crying as he turns the shower on.

I cover my mouth with both my hands feeling tears sting my eyes. Why is he so upset? Did people say things to him at school? I push the door open and walk inside the bathroom. He stops clearing his voice before he speaks.

"Bee?" His voice sounds thick from the crying.

"Alex, what's wrong? Why are you crying?" I walk up to the shower door. He looks through the clear glass at me before more tears leave his eyes. I've never seen him so broken, and it breaks my heart.

"Bee I can't." He cries. I feel a tear roll down my cheek as I open the door. I step into the shower and he takes a step back. "Don't." He tries. I ignore him as my arms wrap around him. I pull me as close to him as our baby will allow. The warm water immediately drenches my clothes, but I don't care. His head rests in the crook of my neck as his arms wrap around me. I feel his body shudder from the cries.

"What happened?"

"School, scouts. I can't Bee." He cries.

"What do you mean?"

"Since you have left school I've been the one getting called names. Getting bullied for knocking my girlfriend up, who happens to be my best friend." He holds me tighter as more tears leave my eyes. I kiss his tattoo letting him know I'm here.

"Bee, they never stop. Even at practice I get picked on, and coach does nothing. He doesn't seem to get any of it. All he wants is to impress the scouts." He gets out. He takes a deep breath before letting out another sob.

"Alex-"

"I've tried to hide it for so long. I love you so much, and this baby so much. I just don't know how to pretend to be okay anymore. The only time I'm actually okay is when I'm with you, or family."

"Oh Alex. I'm sorry." I cry feeling for him. He sighs controlling his cries as he pulls back to look at my face. He cups my cheeks with his hands a small smile on his lips. His eyes are red and puffy.

"You don't have to be sorry. They are right I fucked up. I am a fuck up, and there is no way scouts are going to give a scholarship to a fucked up guy in my situation." I frown at him.

"Alex, don't think like that. Isn't Chris there for you at school? Nini?"

"They are there for me, but they aren't with me all day. Chris and I have gotten into a few fights already because of it. They don't stop." He sniffles. I kiss his lips wanting to distract him from everything. He pulls back resting his forehead on mine.

"I love you." I whisper.

"I love you too, so fucking much." He takes in a deep breath before letting it out. "You should get out before you get sick. You have to stay healthy for you and the baby." He tells me kissing my nose. I nod my head before stepping out of the shower. I shut the door as I grab a towel I wrap it around myself letting it warm me up a little. I walk out only to strip my clothes fast and get warm dry ones on. I put on the outfit I'll wear to dinner.

As I brush my hair Alex comes back out of the bathroom with a towel around his waist. He looks to me taking in my outfit. "Where are you going?"

"We are going to dinner at my parents." He nods his head sighing as he runs a hand down his face.

"Alex?"

"I'm fine. I just wish I had Austin to back me up, even Olivia." He mutters. I frown at him making him shake his head. "What time are we going for dinner?"

"Seven." I smile. He smiles back before walking to his closet. I look to the mirror I sit in front of putting on minimal makeup. By the time I finish putting lipgloss on I feel Alex come back into the room. I turn around only for my mouth to water at how attractive he looks. He rocks the outfit perfectly making me want to just jump him instead of dinner. He clears his throat making my eyes meet his, and he raises an eyebrow at me.

"Do I look okay?" I can only nod my head making him chuckle. I blink my eyes before shaking my head and getting up.

"Okay, time to go to dinner."

--

I smile seeing how happy Alex is to have his family here. He needed this after the time he has been having. I sigh as I watch him walk off with his siblings to another room. "Everything good?" My dad asks sitting next to me. I sigh looking to him.

"School has been rough for him. They were bad with me, and now he gets it all." I tell him honestly. His eyes show concern as he glances where they walked off.

"Why does he stay?" He looks back to me. "Honey, he shouldn't have to go through that."

"I know dad, and I don't know. He just told me about it today. I've never seen him so broken dad." He frowns at me as Justin sits across from him at the table.

"What's up kiddo?" He asks before he frowns from the mood. "What's wrong?" My dad sighs looking to him.

"Your son is getting shit at school, and hasn't said anything." Justin tenses as his hands ball into fists.

"I'm going to kill them. Who? Fucking teenagers that think they know shit." He mutters. I shake my head at him.

"I don't think he wanted me to say anything. So, please don't do anything." I look between both of them. They look to each other for a while before groaning in agreement. "Thank you." I smile. My mom comes in with Nicole by her side.

"Why the hell are you so tense?" Nicole asks rubbing Justin's arm. He shakes his head at her after his eyes meet my pleading ones.

"Nothing babe."

"Where are the others?" My mom asks.

"Tony and Kait went upstairs and Nicole's three went into the other room." My dad shrugs. Alex walks back in with his siblings, and they do not seem that happy. Nicole raises an eyebrow at her kids, but they say nothing.

"What?" Alex asks as he places his hands in the back of my chair. Nicole raises an eyebrow at him.

"What do you mean what? Why did you three just disappear?" She asks. I feel him tense up behind me, and I don't know what to do.

"Mom, don't worry we will fill you in later." Austin easily saves. Alex shoots him a glare making him roll his eyes. "Dude she is going to find out eventually."

"Um what?"

"He thinks the baby is going to take away all his baby brother pluses." She shakes her head at that as my mom tries not to laugh. Alex smacks him upside the head. "Ouch. Dude you will always be my baby brother."

"I hate you." Alex mutters. Austin just grins wrapping his arms around Alex. Alex groans as Austin hugs him tight.

"Love you too, bro."

"Mom, why did you have to have to weird boys." They both gasp looking to Olivia. Nicole shakes her head sighing.

"It's not my fault they take after your father."

"Excuse me!" Justin exclaims.

"You're excused." Nicole smiles.

"Fuck you." Justin mutters.

"Oh you will." Nicole winks. Austin, Olivia, and Alex all gag running out of the room. I cringe in my seat as my parents just roll their eyes.

"You can count on it." Justin grins.

"Okay you two, I think your horny asses need to leave." My mom chuckles.

"Well, if you say so." Justin sighs standing up. Nicole follows his lead as they say bye to everyone before walking out. I groan covering my face with my hands. That was so awkward. Typical Alex's parents.

Chapter twenty nine: the game

I cross my arms pouting as Alex gets on his uniform. I sit in bed feeling terrible, and Alex won't let me get out of bed. "Don't give me that look, bee. I feel bad already."

"But it's the big game." I whine. He rolls his eyes at my words as he puts on a sock over his shin guard on his right leg.

"I know, but for your sake and the baby's you are staying here. Your mom will be here soon too." I gasp as he gives me a guilty look.

"You called her?"

"I didn't want you to be alone, and Nini wanted to watch the game." I groan laying back on the bed. I rub my uncomfortable belly knowing this baby is going to come soon.

"I don't like being baby sat." I frown. I feel the bed shift as he weight is off of it. He walks over to me, and hovers over my body.

"You aren't. It's more like having company so you won't lose your mind." He grins. I can't help but smile back at him. He kisses my lips quick making me pout again. He groans before kissing them again. This time with more passion. "I love you." He whispers on my lips.

"I love you too." I whisper back. He kisses my lips again before a throat being cleared makes him pull back.

"Shouldn't you be off to your big game?" My Mom questions. He mutters something under his breath before grabbing his bag and hurrying out.

"Drive safely!" I call.

"Will do!" I hear him respond just before the door closes. I try to sit up, and do with some time making my mom chuckle. She sits next to me on Alex's side, and looks to me grinning.

"You two are so cute." I shake my head at her before running a hand through my hair.

"Mom." I groan. She just smiles at me before sighing, and getting comfortable on the bed.

"So, what should we do?" She asks. I groan rubbing my stomach feeling uncomfortable. I look down at it frowning. I feel my mom look to me making me look to her. "Getting uncomfortable?" I nod my head.

"Yeah, I'm guessing the baby will be coming sooner than we think." She just grins at that making me raise an eyebrow.

"What?" She questions still looking happy as hell.

"Why does that make you happier?"

"I want to see my grandchild."

--

I forced myself to leave my bed and walk around the apartment. My mom makes dinner knowing the game is almost done, and everyone is going to come over and eat here. "This whole being pregnant thing is not all it's cracked up to be." I mutter sitting at the table.

"I know honey. It was no walk in the park for any of you kids." I sigh looking up at her. She gives me a smile before focusing on the food. I look down to my hands as I start playing with my promise ring on my finger.

Suddenly the door opens as everyone files in. Alex comes straight over to me muttering a hi to my mom. He hugs me and kisses my lips quick making me grin. "How was your time here with your mom?"

"It was nice. The baby is getting uncomfortable though, which makes things annoying." He frowns rubbing my stomach with his right hand before placing a kiss on it. Then he kisses my lips making my smile grow.

"I'm sorry bee. But, soon enough our baby will be here." He grins at me.

"Are you guys ready for that?" Austin asks walking into the room. He wraps his arm around his little brother looking between us both.

"I think so." I say. "I want the baby out of me because it is getting painful."

"Well, I'm okay if the baby needs more time to cook in there." Alex smiles nervously. Austin laughs as I shoot him a playful glare.

"Where's Holly?" I look around trying to see her.

"Oh she has a test this week and needs to study." I nod my head looking down to my stomach bitting my lip. I groan as I feel a weird pain as if I was having a contraction. But it's too early for that, right?

"Babe are you okay?" Alex asks squatting down in front of me. I look into his concern filled eyes knowing mine show some pain.

"I think so." Austin squats down too, and looks at me. He studies my eyes before looking down to the floor. As he looks to the floor I feel a gush as if I just peed myself. My eyes widen as both Alex and Austin look.

"Did your water just break?" Austin asks.

"What?" Alex gasps.

"What's happening?" I hear my mom.

"Her water broke!" Austin exclaims loudly as he jumps up. Alex is frozen in his spot as I just to look my mom fear in my eyes.

"It's going to be all right, honey." She assures me. She pulls Alex up and turns him to look at her. "Go get her bag, and I'll get her to the car." He nods his head hurrying off.

--

Alex's point of view:

It's coming! My baby is coming and I don't think I'm ready. I grab the bag and hurry out of the house. My parents stayed back along with Olivia, but Austin must have gone with bee and her mom. I hurry to the car wanting to get bee to the hospital as fast as we can. As I get in the car next to her I grab her hand. She squeezes mine letting me know she is just as scared as I am.

Today has been so crazy. After the game today I was offered a scholarship, full ride, to a school in town. I talked to the coach about the situation I'm in, and he seemed to be totally understanding. He knew what I wanted and is willing to give it to me. I didn't even get to tell bee about it because the baby decided it wants to come out.

As soon as we get to the hospital I'm carrying Bianca in as Austin follows while Jade, bee's mom, parks. He is shouting that bee is in labor, and the nurses jump into action. They get a wheelchair for her, and I help her sit in it. Then we are rushed down the hall to a room. As she is wheeled into the room Austin stops me turning me towards him. His hands on my shoulders.

"Congrats bro. I'll be here, but I'm the lobby until it's safe to come in." He smiles at me. I nod my head processing his words. "Now go comfort your girl." He smirks pushing me towards the room.

I gulp walking in seeing her hooked up to machines. She smiles at me gesturing for me to come over with her hands. I walk over practically shaking out of my skin. I'm going to be a father in just hours. I'm going to be able to hold my little baby in my arms.

There is going to be a tiny person that needs me to care for them. Provide for them. They are going to become my world, along with Bianca.

Chapter thirty: Maddison Elizabeth

I groan trying to get comfortable in this hospital bed, but find it hard. I keep my eyes closed wanting to sleep longer but a crying snaps them open. I look to see Alex try to calm our little baby. He holds the baby close to him as he paces the room bouncing them slightly. I smile at the sight as he tries to stop the cries.

Our little baby is wrapped in the hospital's white blanket with blue and pink stripes by the end. "Let me feed her." I say. Alex turns to me slightly startled before nodding his head. He walks over placing our little princess in my arms. As she starts to feed I look up to Alex grinning.

"You did an amazing job." He kisses my lips. I look down at my little girl grinning before pressing a kiss to her forehead. I look back up to Alex as it all hits me.

"We made this."

"We did, and I'm damn proud of it. I got my queen over here, and now my princess." The happiness rolls off him filling me completely.

"You should go tell the others. They are probably dying to meet our little princess." I sigh looking down to my little girl, who is happily feeding.

"I'll get them, but only after she eats." I look to Alex giving him a pointed look.

"Just go tell them about her, that's all I meant." He sighs nodding his head. He kisses my lips before he kisses Maddison's head. He reluctantly leaves the room to go fill our family in. It all happened so fast there wasn't time to tell them along the way what was happening.

Maddison let's go and fusses, so I start to burp her. After a little bit she burps, and I bring her to the other boob. She latches on happily making me smile. I fix the hospital gown to cover my other side. I watch her eat mesmerized that she was growing inside of me. Alex and I created this beautiful little baby. This little baby in my arms is my world, and nothing is going to change that.

The door opens to Alex groaning as our family follows him in. He gives me a sorry look making me smile laughing at him. "They wouldn't stay."

"Let me see my grandbaby." I hear my mom. She pushes her way through as my dad follows her.

"Hold on Mom, she's still eating."

"What's her name?" I look to see Austin, who looks about to explode with excitement.

"Maddison Elisabeth." I grin. Everyone awes at her name making me look to Alex proud. He shares the same look pride in his eyes. Maddison fussed making me pull her away to burp her, and Alex quickly covers me up. I burp my little girl, and pull her away from my shoulder to look at her. I look into her blue eyes, just like her daddy. They blink looking at me before she coos, and looks over seeing Alex. Her mouth forms an O before she seems to smile.

"Can I hold her now?" I hear my mom beg. I smile a laugh escaping my lips before looking to her.

"Yes Mom, here she is." I gently hand my princess to her. She eagerly takes her and tries not to squeal with happiness as she holds her granddaughter.

"Oh god." My dad gasps.

"What? What's wrong?" Alex and I ask at the same time. My heart races in my chest fear rising.

"I'm a grandfather."

"Damn, that just hit me too. I'm a grandfather, and I'm going to be a dad again. Fuck." Justin mutters looking over my mom's shoulder. I let out a breath knowing my daughter is fine. I hold back a laugh as Nicole smacks the back of Justin's head.

"Don't swear in front of the baby." She scolds him. He groans rubbing the back of his head.

"She doesn't know what I said." He tries.

"Still innocent ears." My dad says shooting Justin a glare. Justin rolls his eyes before walking over, and hugging Alex before myself. I happily hug him back.

"Congratulations you two."

"Thank you." I grin as he pulls away.

--

A cry wakes me up making me jump ready to help my little princess. I scan the hospital room only to see Alex already getting to her. I smile at the as I force myself to get up off the bed. I take small steps towards them as Alex picks her up, and tries to sooth her crying. "Do you need daddy to change you?" He asks her in a soft voice. She continues to cry making him sigh.

"You can try that." I offer. He jumps slightly his head turning to me.

"You scared me. What if I dropped her?" I roll my eyes at him.

"You won't drop her. Now change her and then I'll feed her." I smile at him. He smiles back making him look irresistible. I kiss his cheek before heading back to the bed. I sit with my legs criss crossed waiting to feed my baby. Alex changes her taking his time to do it right. I try not to laugh at him talking himself through it. Maddison still cries the whole time making my heart hurt.

"Alex, hurry up she's hungry." I whine.

"I know, I'm sorry this is the first time I'm doing it myself." He says as he wraps her back up in the blanket. He brings her over as I take the top of the gown down. I take her in my arms and she laches on instantly. I smile down at her before looking up to Alex.

"Have you slept?" I ask taking in his tired features. He shakes his head looking guilty making me raise an eyebrow at him. "Why not?"

"What if something happens to my queen or princess?" He asks. I smile at him knowing he is just overly worried now.

"We will be fine, Alex, and you need your sleep. If you don't sleep how are you suppose to help Maddison and I?" He sighs sitting on the bed as he faces me.

"I know, but I can't help but freak out. Instead of one person to protect and worry about I have two."

"I know, but just think all parents do it. You can talk to your dad too if you are still super worried." He just nods his head before leaning forward and placing a kiss on my forehead. I pout looking into his eyes making him confused.

"What's wrong?"

"I want a kiss on the lips." Alex chuckles before his lips meet mine. I smile against his lips making him smile too.

"I love you."

"I love you too." I whisper back against his lips.

Chapter thirty one: wait what?

"No, they are not coming over." I narrow my eyes on Alex. He frowns at me pouting his lips making me hold in the urge to kiss him.

"Why not?"

"Last time they couldn't stay quiet and woke Maddison up." I point out. I can see the wheels in his head turning as he remembers it happening.

"They won't be loud I promise." He pleads. I roll my eyes at his pleas. I take the bottle from Maddison's mouth as I notice she is done suckling. I start to burp her as I ignore her father, who is acting like a child.

"You said the same thing last time." I point out. He groans before sliding to the floor dramatically from the chair he was sitting in. I raise an eyebrow at him as I hear our little girl burp.

"I promise it won't happen again." I shake my head at him as I cradle Maddison in my arms.

"Why can't you just go out with them instead?" I question growing annoyed with his childish behavior. He gives me a pointed look as he gets back in his chair.

"It's not the same, and they want to see Maddison." He gives me a sheepish smile. I bite my lip hearing that looking down to her. I barely have let anyone outside of the family hold her. I don't want anyone to hurt her or take her from me.

"Who?"

"Some teammates?" I give him a dirty look.

"The same members who tried causing shit between us?"

"No, just my close buddies on the team. You know them. We used to chill with them after some of the games." Alex tries his puppy dog eyes on me.

"Alex, we have a baby. Why are you acting like a child?" He just grins at me.

"Does this mean they can come?"

"I want names." I tell him giving him a look before standing to change Maddison as she starts to fuss and smell.

"Chris, and he's obviously bringing Nini for you. Then there is Mark, Derrick, and Billy." I nod my head as I head to her room. I feel Alex follow me, which I don't mind as I lay my baby on the changing table.

"As long as they can behave themselves. Also if you can get me Chinese that would be amazing. I've been wanting that all day." I smile at the thought of food.

"Um Bee, you aren't pregnant again are you?" I roll my eyes even though I know he can't see it.

"Alex, first off we haven't had sex since before she was born. Second off, I'm still not healed from her. So, cut me some slack and get me my damn Chinese food." I snap at him. He jumps hurrying out of the room. Idiot, thinking I'm pregnant right now. I'm just moody as hell and I can't help it.

"Sorry for that princess." I smile looking down to my little girl. I finish wiping her before putting the new diaper on. I clip her onesie back together before picking my smiling princess up. She watches me happily cooing as I grab her diaper, and put it in the trash on the way out. I put her in the swing before going to the kitchen sink. I can still see her as I wash my hands.

"Just called the food place, they'll bring it in 20. Also the guys will be over in 10." Alex calls before picking Maddison up. He grins kissing her face before bringing her into the kitchen with me.

--

As soon as I hear her cry I march out to find the culprit. Nini and I were just getting some snacks for the guys. They can't keep my daughter for two minutes before she cries. As soon as I see them all they all seem alarmed. Alex holds her bouncing her gently to try to calm her. "Babe, I think she's hungry." Alex says looking to me.

"Let me have her." I say going to grab her. Alex hands her over with no question. I smile at my little girl as she stops crying.

"What?"

"She just wanted her mom." Nini laughs. I smile before walking back to the kitchen with Nini following me. "So," she starts sitting at the counter stop. I look to her as my princess quiets down.

"What?"

"Has Alex talked to you yet?" She whispers. I raise an eyebrow at her glancing to the area the guys are.

"What do you mean?"

"I'll take that as a no." She looks guiltily down at the counter.

"Nini, can you hold Maddison?" I ask walking towards her. She looks up grinning, and opens her arms up.

"Yes, of course." I smile giving her Maddison. I walk out, only after knowing she is safe, and walk towards Alex. He looks up at me meeting my eyes and stands right away. I can tell by the look on his face he can read mine knowing I want to talk.

"Guys I'll be right back." Alex walks to me, taking my hand and taking me to our bedroom. He shuts the door before facing me.

"What?" I ask. He raises an eyebrow.

"What do you mean, what? You wanted to talk." I sigh shaking my head.

"What are you hiding from me." He bites his lip as he thinks. I can see it click in his eyes.

"Did Nini say something?" I nod my head making him let out a long breath. "Chris and I are making a business. We are making tee shirts, sweatshirts, and hats. We finally finalized the idea." My eyes widen. I was not expecting to hear that for an answer.

"Wait, what?" He bites his lips rubbing the back of his neck.

"Yeah, that's what the meetings have been about." I just nod my head processing it.

"And you haven't told me until now because...?" I ask curiously.

"Wasn't sure what was going to happen with it." He shrugs nervously. I smile at him and wrap my arms around him for a hug.

"I'm proud of you babe." I say before kissing his lips quick. He grins as his arms wrap tightly around me. He kisses me back happy I'm on his side with this. Why wouldn't I be?

"Dude you coming back!" We hear Mark call. I laugh as Alex groans.

"Yeah, I'm coming." He answers back loudly before he kisses me and walks back. I walk back to the kitchen to see Nini cradling Maddison in her arms.

"Is it bad that this makes me want one?" She asks looking up to me.

"I wouldn't do that now. Nini it might look like we got our shit together, but it's a struggle." Nini gives me a pointed look before rolling her eyes.

"Yeah, okay." She rolls her eyes. "But what if I told you I was having one?" She questions looking nervous now. I look to her confused making her bite her lip. I take Maddison from her needing to hold her.

"Um what?" She gets down and goes in her bag before giving me a gift. My eyebrows furrows looking at the gift box. I put Maddison in the swing in the kitchen before going back to the gift. I open it and my jaw drops seeing the positive pregnancy test. I look up to Nini with watery eyes only to see her with the same look. I hug her tight not being able to say anything.

"I'm here for you hun, and everything will be okay." I assure her.

"I don't know how to tell Chris." She whispers.

"You haven't told him?" I ask pulling away.

"No, I'm scared. I know I said I want one and all, but it's like actually happening."

"I know hun. Let's put it back in the box and get his ass in here." Her eyes widen at my words.

"B-"

"Chris!" I call cutting her off as I put it back in the box. She bites her lip in fear.

"What?"

"Can you come into the kitchen for a second?"

"No, please not yet." Nini begs. I sigh hiding the gift.

"What's up?" Chris asks walking into the room. I look to him smiling, but he frowns looking to Nini. "Babe what's wrong?" She shakes her head.

"Nothing, just wanted you to bring the food out to the guys." He raises an eyebrow knowing that she is hiding something. He ignores it though as he nods his head, and takes the food from the counter.

"Thank you." I smile. He nods his head before walking off. Maddison fusses again making me take a deep breath before picking her up. I walk over to the guys, Nini following me.

"What's wrong with princess?" Alex asks.

"She needs to be changed, can you do it this time?" He smiles nodding his head. He stands up taking her and heads off to her room to change her. "Thank you babe."

"Wow never thought he'd be so whipped. He seems to be a good dad though." Billy says.

"He is." I grin.

Chapter thrity two: finally did it

I finish feeding Maddison, and burp her before placing her on the bed. I fix my shirt before picking her up, and kissing her head. I smile cradling her in my arms. "Awe my little princess." She coos with her mouth open. She looks to me and looks like she is smiling.

The door opens and I hear it slam shit before feet running to the bedroom. "Where are my girls?" I hear Alex call excitedly. I laugh at his excitement.

"In our room." I call out. Alex races in before jumping on he bed. I narrow my eyes on him because of how he did that with Maddison on the bed. "Alex!" I scold.

"It's up!" He shouts.

"What is?"

"The website." He grins ready to burst in complete excitement.

"Really? Awe Alex I'm so happy for you." I grin leaning over to kiss his lips. He kisses me back carefully because of Maddison in my arms. I pull back and look into his bright eyes.

"Yes, it's actually happening. I can't believe it." I laugh at him looking down to Maddison. She watches Alex unsure of what to make of him right now. Alex looks to her taking her from me. He lifts her in the air before bringing her to his face and kissing her.

"Daddy did it princess." She seems to grin at him as she grabs at his head. He laughs kissing her again.

"Careful she just ate." I warn. He nods his head before placing her on the bed. She reaches for him, and he lowers his head to her.

"We should celebrate, and Chris and Nini can join us." Alex gushes happily as he kisses Maddison's face after every word. I laugh shaking my head at him.

"Okay Alex." I sigh as he puts Maddison in her swing in our room. He turns around grinning at me. "Go call Chris." I tell him as he dives onto the bed. He takes his phone out, and calls Chris. Just as he hits call my phone rings. I wave him out making his eyes roll, but he leaves as I pick my phone up.

"Hello." I smile knowing its Nini.

"I told him." She sounds scared making me grow serious.

"What did he do? What did he say?" I start asking worrying about my best friends' relationship. She takes a long breath before letting it out slowly, and I just wait patiently for her to speak.

"He went silent, and hasn't spoken to me. He went to the bathroom and hasn't come out. Bianca, I don't know what to do." I can hear the tears in her voice making me frown.

"Alex should be talking to him right now, so maybe he can talk some sense into him. I'm sorry that he went silent hun. I really am. Alex questioned me if it was his when I told him, so at least it's not that reaction." I try to be supportive and positive.

"I guess, but what if he leaves me? I can't Bianca, I really can't." She cries.

"Breathe Nini, Chris won't do that. You just have to give him a little time."

"I guess, but still."

"Nini, this a life changing thing. It's going to take time for him to cope with it."

"Okay, he's coming out. I got to go." She quickly hangs up. I frown as I put my phone down. Alex walks in still talking on the phone, so I stay quiet as I look to Maddison.

"Dude, man the fuck up and own up to it. That shit ain't going to fly anymore." I see Maddison looking right at me as she starts to move like crazy. She fusses making her face scrunch up, and I am quick to get up off the bed to get to her. I pick up my little Maddison and hold her close to me as I bounce her slightly. I turn to look at Alex, who is looking annoyed.

"Chris, go talk to her. She's probably scared shitless because of your reaction." I raise an eyebrow at him, and his eyes meet mine for a second before looking to Maddison.

"Don't worry you got time, and it's the best thing ever." Alex assures Chris. "Now go talk to her, and be here at six." Alex orders him before hanging up and letting out a dramatic sigh as he falls onto the bed. He looks up to me making me hold back a smile.

"So, I'm guessing Nini already told you." Alex states, and I nod my head.

"Yes she did, and I'm guessing Chris told you because he freaked." Alex sighs nodding his head.

"Yup. He can't get his head around the fact he is going to be a father now."

"Well it's something to process. I mean you didn't think she was yours." I point out. Alex groans covering his face with his hands.

"Don't bring that up." He groans. Maddison fusses grabbing my baby hair that fell from my bun.

"Ow baby." I grown. Alex gets up to help pry her hand off. "Take her." I tell Alex, and he does without question. He kisses her head as I walk to the bathroom needing to pee. After I do my business I walk back out to see Alex on the bed with Maddison on his chest. Her eyes close after they spot me, and she smiles a little smile.

"Alex?" He looks over to me careful not to let her move.

"What's up bee?"

"I love you." He smiles at me his eyes shining with love.

"I love you too." He carefully gets up putting a sleepy Maddison in her crib. I raise an eyebrow at him as he hurries over to me. His arms wrap around me as his lips find mine. I kiss him back my eyes closing. We each put our love into the kiss wanting to prove our love to the other. There is a knock on the door making us groan pulling apart.

I walk to go get it, and I can feel Alex follow me out. I look through the peep hole before opening the door. Olivia stands there and smiles at us. "How did you get in?" Alex asks.

"Don't worry about that." She waves. I move aside to let her in, and she walks right in heading to the kitchen. I shut the door before looking to Alex raising an eyebrow. He just sighs shaking his head before walking after her.

"Um sis?" Alex asks. She sighs and turns to look at him.

"I'm not staying home right now with Mom. She is crazy." She says. I laugh shaking my head. "I just wish the baby was out already."

"You don't have that much longer." I smile. Maddison fusses making Alex and I share a look. I raise an eyebrow at him making him sigh before he heads to go get her. I smile at that before looking to Olivia.

"I still got about a month. And I just got out of school." She whines. I shake my head at her.

"You know I have a daughter right? I know what it's like to be the crazy hormonal lady. You can deal with it." I sigh. She shrugs still looking for food.

Chapter thirty three: life

After we forced Olivia to leave we only had twenty minutes before Chris and Nini got here. I groan as Maddison fusses again from where she lays on her play mat. Alex is quick to get to her just as she starts to cry. He picks her up and rocks her in his arms. I walk into the kitchen to find something for all of us to eat when they get here. I see somethings that I can make, so I grab all the ingredients.

"Need any help?" I hear Alex as I start setting up. I look over my shoulder at him, and he stands in the doorway feeding Maddison.

"Nope, you got her. That's all the help I need right now." I smile.

"What are you making?" Alex asks coming into the kitchen.

"Chicken parmigiana." I say as I start to prep the chicken.

"Sounds delicious." I feel him step right next to me making me on edge.

"Alex." I warn making him chuckle.

"What? I'm just watching what you do, and so is princess over here." I bite my lip as I continue to make dinner. The whole time Alex is right there next to me, and Maddison watches everything with her big eyes. After I put a pot of water to boil for the pasta the buzzer sounds.

"They're here." I say looking to Alex. He nods his head, and I take Maddison from him. I hold her on my hip still holding her close. I hold her away from the stove as I peek in the oven for the chicken. Seeing it is almost done I close it before stepping away with Maddison.

"Where are your girls?" I hear Chris.

"In the kitchen." Alex says proudly. My heart flutters hearing him talk like that.

"Smells good in here." Nini says entering the kitchen. I smile at her as I make my way over.

"It's good to see you hun." I hug her with one arm.

"You too." She sighs before pulling away. "Need any help?"

"Can you hold her?" I ask, and she takes her gently out of my hold. She holds Maddison to her chest as she watches me. I go to check the chicken again, and see I have to take them out. The water also starts boiling, but I still take the chicken out first. I put the two pans on the cutting board before I put the pasta in.

--

"I can't believe it's up already." Chris says bouncing Maddison lightly with his knee, which he has her sitting on. He holds her safely, but I still watch them cautiously.

"I know, dude. We've been working on this for so long." Alex chimes in.

"So, how are you two doing?" I ask. We didn't talk that much durning dinner, other than everyone talking about school. Alex was going on about how happy he was that the coach still let him play even when he did online schooling. They still have their last game of the season this Friday, which is the second biggest game of the season. Chris and Nini share a look before looking between Alex and I.

"Well I'm guessing you know." Chris says looking to me.

"That depends on what you are thinking." He rolls his eyes.

"The baby."

"Oh yeah I do." I smile at them before giving him a pointed look. "And what do you think of it?"

"Um I don't know. It's still new and confusing, but I'm a little excited." He says smiling looking at Nini. "I'm mean this little princess is so damn cute, and seems pretty easy." Alex and I look at each other.

"Um dude, it's not all that easy." Alex says looking back to Chris.

"I know, but you make it look easy." He breathes. I look at him smiling as I lean my head on Alex's shoulder. Nini sits next to Chris, who still holds Maddison.

"So, what do you two plan to do?" Alex asks.

"Well, our parents still don't know. So, we have to tell them." Nini sighs biting her lip.

"We'll obviously need to find a place together by the time the baby comes. And then there is fucking graduation coming up in a couple weeks."

"Chris!" The three of us shout at him. He cringes knowing he swore in front of Maddison.

"Sorry princess." He kisses her head. She just smiles looking towards him. She then looks to me, and reaches out trying to grab me. I laugh as I take her from Chris.

"Hi my princess." I say in a baby voice as I kiss her cheeks. She grins at me her big eyes taking me in.

"Everything will come together in time. I would tell your parents though." Alex says. I look to see them nod their heads in agreement.

"We plan to this weekend. I just don't know what they will say or do." Chris grabs Nini's hand with his.

"It's nerve racking, but it might not be as bad as you think." I try.

"We'll have to see. I guess the future is now here."

"Yeah, first the website and now your are a father to be and I'm a father. Wow."

"Shit." Nini smacks the back of Chris' head making him groan looking at her. "Sorry."

"Don't say sorry to me, say sorry to her." He sighs.

"Sorry her." We all crack up laughing, and so does Maddison.

"Congratulations by the way." I smile at them.

"Yeah, Congratulations you two." Alex says wrapping an arm around me.

"Thank you guys. At least we already got two people on our side."

\- \-

"Queen!" I stay quiet in the shower not wanting to get out. I hear the bathroom door open, but I ignore it. "I know you can hear me." Alex says amused.

"I don't want to get out yet." I whine. I watch him roll his eyes as he gets up to the glass door.

"I want to celebrate." He frowns. I raise an eyebrow at him.

"How?"

"You know." He winks at me. "Awe you're blushing." I hide my face not wanting him to see it.

"Stop." I drag.

"Come celebrate with me." I smile looking to him before someone pops in my head. "Princess is asleep." He says as if reading my mind. I smile happy to hear before I turn the water off. Alex grins making me laugh as I open the door. I step out and wrap myself in a towel just before Alex picks me up. He puts me over his shoulder before making his way to the bedroom.

My back hits the sheets and I laugh looking up to him grinning. He grins back before his lips meet mine. Claiming them as his, and mine respond back with the same sense of claiming. This boy is my everything just like Maddison is, and I wouldn't have it any other way. I love him so much, and I know tonight he won't do anything other that make love to me. I smile against his lips happy as hell to be with him.

Chapter thrity four:
Cassidy and a suprise

I groan hearing Alex's phone ring. I open my eyes to see he is still sleeping. I give him a shove making him just open his eyes. He then grabs his phone, and before he can answer the call Maddison starts crying. I glare at Alex, who gives me a innocence look, as I get up to go stop our daughter from crying.

I pick her up and cradle her to my chest. I bounce her a little to get her to calm down. Alex jumps out of bed alarmed before he hangs up. "What's wrong?"

"My Mom just went to the hospital, the baby is coming." My eyes widen. We weren't ready to hear this yet. Let alone ready for our baby to have an aunt or uncle that is younger than her.

"Are you going to go?" I question sitting on the bed with Maddison. Alex sighs sitting down facing me.

"I don't know. Should I?" He asks looking down to Maddison.

"It's up to you. If you want to wait to go tomorrow you can do that. She isn't getting her shots until the following day, so I'm not bringing her. I'll ask Nini to watch her tomorrow, so I can go."

"You don't have to." Alex says. "I'll wait until they have news on if the baby is here." He yawns.

"Are you sure?" I yawn.

"Yeah I'm tried, and I rather not sleep in a hospital chair."

"Fair point." I smile looking down to Maddison.

"Is princess sleeping again?" I watch her eyes close as she relaxes taking even breathes. I nod my head as I stand up with her before putting her back in her bassinet. I turn around to look at Alex, who is laying back down. I crawl into bed laying next to him.

"What do you think it is?" I ask as he wraps his arms around me.

"I can't even think about that right now." He mumbles into my hair. I sigh hugging him so we are both wrapped in each other's arms.

- -

I get off the phone with Chris making sure Nini, Maddison, and him are okay. I have never left her before and I don't like it. Alex has his arms around me as we stand in the waiting room with his siblings. We wait to hear about their new sibling.

"When do you think Dad will come out?" Austin asks. He holds Holly on his lap close to him. She laughs looking at him over her shoulder. I'm happy he has her. The last relationship he was in ended badly leaving him heartbroken for a while.

"Are you whining?" She asks. He pouts looking down.

"No." Olivia snorts.

"Bullshit." She calls. Austin rolls his eyes just as Justin walks through the doors. We all hurry over to meet him. He smiles at us all, but he looks really tired.

"What is it?" Austin asks eagerly.

"A girl."

"Well damn. Looks like little Maddison has an aunt that is younger than her." Austin says looking to Alex and I. Holly smacks him on the head making him groan.

"Austin, really? I just have a newborn, and I don't need a five year old too." Justin groans. "Come on you guys, time to meet her."

"What's her name?" I ask smiling.

"Cassidy." Justin grins. We fallow him into the room to see little Cassidy. Nicole sits in the bed as she finishes changing Alex's little sister. Nicole looks up and grins at us just as the door closes.

"Hey kids, come meet the new member of the family." She says as she picks Cassidy up.

"I don't know what to do." Alex whispers to me. I smile looking up to him. He looks to me completely unsure.

"Just go see your sister."

"But it's weird." He whispers.

"Why?"

"She is younger than my daughter."

"Bro, we can hear you." Austin chuckles.

"Yeah you suck at whispering." Olivia laughs. His cheeks turn pink as he looks to the ground.

"Sorry."

"There is nothing to be sorry for Alex. I know it's weird, and trust me it's weird for your father and I too." Nicole says. "But come here and hold your sister." He smiles a little smile as he follows her order.

- -

We get back home only to be met with a knock on the door five minutes after we walked in. Alex groans before opening it up, and he stands there shocked. "Ethan? Nate?" I walk to the door leaving Nini and Chris in the kitchen with Maddison.

"Hello to you too." I hear that familiar voice. I get to the door my eyes widening. There stands Uncle Zach and Aunt Lissa's two older sons. Ethan is our age and Nate is one younger.

"Hey guys." I smile at them.

"Bianca!" They light up tackling me in hugs. I laugh as I hug them back.

"Guys get off her." Alex warns. We haven't seen them in three years because their parents had to leave for business.

"Easy bro." Ethan chuckles as they get off me.

"Word on the street is you two live here now." Nate says as he walks right past us. They both look around taking in our place. I hear Maddison cry making me hurry to her, and I take her from Nini.

"Ethan, Nate? Is that you?" Chris asks walking out of the kitchen. I hear them all catching up as I look to Nini nervously.

"They don't know about princess, here." I say nodding towards Maddison. Nini looks over my shoulder before looking to me.

"It'll be fine. Breathe Bianca, and just think they were bound to find out anyway." She tries. I sigh nodding my head. We walk out of the kitchen, with me cradling Maddison in my arms. She stops her fussing as she looks around the room to see new faces.

"You're babysitting?" Nate asks his eyes watching me closely. Ethan raises an eyebrow at me before his eyes study Maddison.

"Oh shit, that's your baby!" Ethan exclaims. "Who the hell is the father?"

"He better be sticking around." Nate adds. I look to Alex trying to hold back a smile.

"Guys, Maddison is our baby." Alex says wrapping his arms around me. Ethan and Nate share a look before Nate groans. He reaches in his pocket and pulls out his wallet. Nate pulls ten dollars out and hands them to Ethan, who snatched it quickly.

"Um... What was that?" Nini asks the question we all have.

"Nate didn't think Alex and Bianca would get together. I did, so we bet on it." Ethan shrugs easily.

"You bet on us?" Alex says faking hurt.

"Well, Nate thought Chris and Nini would get together." I look with wide eyes between them before looking to Chris and Nini. Chris stands with one arm around her waist holding her to his side protectively.

"Oh right, ten dollars." Nate says holding his hand out.

"Damnit I should have kept my mouth shut." Ethan forcefully put the money on Nate's hand.

"Damn, you bet on us too. I honestly don't know what to say to that."
Chris sighs pulling Nini closer to him. I look at the two boys who could be
twins in looks. They both look just like their father, but with their mother's
brown eyes and light brown hair color.

"You two haven't changed a bit." I grin fixing Maddison so she sits on my
hip, and I still hold her close to me.

"Looks like everything else has." Ethan chuckles.

"I guess so." I shrug.

"You have a baby for crying out loud." Nate exclaims. Maddison starts to
cry making me look to Alex, who takes her easily.

"Shh princess, everything is okay." Alex bounces her a he walks to the
bedroom to change her.

"So, how long has this been a thing?" Ethan asks lounging on the couch.
Nate chills right next to him putting his feet on his brother's lap. Chris
takes one of the chairs, and pulls Nini to sit on his lap.

"What? The baby?" I ask sitting in the other chair.

"Well, first you and Alex." Ethan clarifies.

"Yeah I thought you didn't like him that way." Nate adds. Chris laughs, and
so does Nini.

"Oh they have loved each other since day one of laying eyes on each other."

"Oh I remember." Ethan laughs, and Nate does to agreeing to how we
acted.

"What made you want to try for that little princess?" Nate asks smoothly.
I sigh as I retie my hair into a messy bun.

"She wasn't planned. She was a surprise."

"Damn guess we missed a lot." I roll my eyes at that as Alex comes back with Maddison. He hold her as she sits facing all of us, and his right arm supports her. He holds her on his right side as he is on his phone with the other. I smile seeing them which makes Ethan and Nate gag.

"Cassidy won't stop crying." Alex sighs getting off the phone.

"Babies do that." Nini says.

"Who has a baby?" Nate asks.

"Oh my parents just had another baby." Alex says.

"Damn." Ethan draws.

"Oh yeah, you guys missed a lot." Chris chuckles.

Chapter thirty five: moody days

- -

"Dude, that's so cheating!" I glare at Ethan.

"No, I won fair and square." Alex goes point to the screen.

"You're just mad you lost." Chris laugh.

"He clearly cheated. No one can get that many kills." Ethan tries. His voice is so loud which I glare at him for. I just put Maddison down for a nap.

"If you don't shut up you are all leaving." I state. They all look to me with guilty looks.

"Sorry, Queen." Alex says quietly. I smile at that looking to Nini who is trying not to laugh.

"Why is there nothing to eat in here?" Nate calls loudly. I groan getting up hearing Maddison cry.

"He better be out by the time I get back in here." I glare at Alex. I walk off to go get Maddison to stop her crying. I pick her up kissing her head.

"What's wrong princess?" I ask in a baby voice. She still cries making me frown. I hold her close bouncing her a little. She got her shots yesterday, and has been tired and fussy ever since.

"Alex!" I call as I walk out of the room to where everyone is. Nate looks to me with pleading eyes. He even drops to his knees, but I ignore him.

"What's wrong?" Alex asks.

"You idiots woke her up."

"We didn't mean to." Ethan rushed out. I roll my eyes taking a seat.

"Whatever, Alex give me that blanket." He jumps into action handing me the blanket. I use it as a cover as I breast feed Maddison in the room.

"Um Bianca?" I raise an eyebrow at Ethan.

"What is the issue? Play your damn game." I state annoyed. He bites his lip looking to Alex.

"Um queen, why in front of everyone?"

"No one can see anything. Nate what the hell are you doing?" I ask looking to him. He looks between all the guys before looking to me.

"Please don't kick me out!" He begs. I roll my eyes.

"Just go get some food. I want chicken lo mein." I tell him. He looks to Alex not knowing what to do.

"Well go, what are you looking at me for?"

"Um... Bianca your not pregnant again right?" Chris asks. I snap my head to him shocked.

"Why would you think that?" His hands go up showing no harm.

"Nothing, never mind." Nini smacks him in the back of the head. Alex gives me a look though, and I give him a pointed one.

"Alex really? When was the last time we had sex?" I asked him. His cheeks tint pink making me smile.

"TMI! I didn't need to hear that!" Ethan shouts.

"Shut up Ethan." I snap at him. He gulps sliding from his seat to the floor. I shake my head at his childish behavior. I feel Maddison stop nursing, and I look to see she is asleep again. I smile at her before looking to Alex.

"Is she sleeping again?" He asks.

"Yeah can you take her without waking her? I have to fix my shirt." He nods his head coming over to carefully take her. Once he has her without making me flash everyone, and have her wake up. He walks her to the bedroom and puts her back to bed. He comes back out just as I toss the blanket next to me as I already fixed my shirt.

"And for your information I'm just PMSing." I inform sighing. I hear Chris and Ethan makes gagging noises making me roll my eyes.

"Oh grow up guys." Alex rolls his eyes.

- -

"How are you feeling?" Alex asks as he holds me close. Maddison is sleeping, and Alex and I are in bed ready to sleep.

"What do you mean?" I ask holding him closer to me as I tighten my right arm around him more.

"From earlier with the guys." He says as one hand goes to run his fingers through my hair.

"Yeah I'm fine. I just get a little moody the week before I get my period."

"I know, it's just been a while." He sighs as his hands pause for a second. "Bianca?" At the seriousness in his voice my heart races, and my body freezes. Not to mention that he said my actual name.

"Yes?" My voice is nothing more than a whisper as the fear of the unknown floods me.

"When do you think you want to have another?" He asks gently. I blink at his question before moving my head to look up at him. Our eyes meet as his hand pauses again, but this time for a longer time.

""What?" I ask just blinking. His eyes shy away as they flicker to the bassinet that is across the room. To be honest I never thought about having a second. I want to say it's because Maddison is still so little, but in reality it's because I never even thought of the first one.

"Never mind." He says. I can feel him let out a long breath, and his eyes seem to show less brightness than before. I roll to be on my stomach, but half on Alex. I look him in the eyes as my hands cup his face.

"You just caught me off guard." I assure him as he looks me in the eyes. "Honestly I never thought about it. We just had Maddison, and I don't think I'm ready to have another baby right now." I kiss his lips making his turn into a smile.

"I didn't mean to throw you off." He chuckles.

"I know." I grin.

"So, like a year?" I bite my lip thinking about it. I mean I don't want them to have a big age gap, and if we start trying in a year it might take longer. At the same time a year sounds good enough to me.

"Yeah, a year." He grins kissing my lips.

"One thing though." He says making me furrow my eyebrows. I cock my head to the side as my eyes still look into his.

"What?"

"Can we still practice?" He asks innocently making me laugh. I stop as I look to the bassinet not wanting to wake Maddison up.

"Yes we can still practice." He grins at that before he flips us over.

"Good, I need to work on my skills." He whispers before his lips are on mine. I smile against his as my arms wrap around his neck. I pull him close as he settles between my legs.

Chapter thirty six: game day

I groan walking out of the bathroom with my hands slightly wet still. Alex chuckles from where he sits on his laptop at the table. Maddison is in the swing just across from him with sleepy eyes. "Why are you laughing?" My hand rests on my lower stomach as the cramps still haven't gone away.

"Nothing." He is quick to recover.

"Yeah I know it's been awhile." I sigh taking a seat next to him, in front of my laptop. We are finishing up our last assignments for high school. This way we can graduate with our class at the end of next week. They even gave caps and gowns to us. Tonight is the teams last game, and Alex is playing.

"You got that right. Oh, the basketball coach said some schools are looking at my numbers." He says in slight annoyance.

"You wanted to play both sports." I point out. He gives me a look as he slouches back in his seat.

"I know, but I didn't expect to the that good with both." I roll my eyes as I glance over to Maddison.

"Which one would up play in college?" I ask.

"I've already talked with a soccer coach at the college that's just twenty minutes away. He said it's fine if I'm not living on campus."

"I know that, but if you don't want to play soccer then look at your options with basketball." He groans at my words making me shake my head. I groan too as cramps come back.

"Queen I all ready signed with the soccer one." I shrug my shoulders.

"I was only saying." He sighs nodding his head.

"I know." He looks to the time on his laptop before he groans. "I have to start getting ready in five." I smile shaking my head at him.

"Why do you seem so annoyed?" He just gives me a pointed look. I raise an eyebrow at his look.

"It's the last game." He frowns. I try to hold in my laughter, but with little success.

"Just finish your last assignment and go get ready."

—

Alex left to go for warm ups five minutes ago. My meds have finally kicked in for the cramps, so I don't feel them anymore. I pick Maddison up smiling at her cute little soccer outfit. She has a little red bow on a headband around her head, which matches with her onesie. She has on a white onesie with red writing saying Daddy's Princess, and between the words is a heart that looks like a soccer ball. The sleeves are long keeping her arms covered.

I put her in the her car seat as Nini grabs the diaper bag. "Are we ready?" She asks as her keys jingle in her hand.

"Yes." I smile as I pick up the car seat. I wear Alex's away jersey and Nini wears Chris'. We walk out of the apartment, with me locking the door before we head to the car. After I give Nini the car seat I put the plastic bottom the car seat clicks in in the car. I make sure it's in there right and won't move. Once it is good I put Maddison in.

"Are his parents going to be there?" Nini asks as I get in the passenger seat.

"I think his dad is coming. They didn't want to being Cassidy out to this kind of event." Nini nods the car agreeing as she turns out to the road. "How are you feeling?" I ask looking to her.

"As of right now pretty good. I don't feel that nauseous in the morning. I have been more tired though." She shrugs.

"Yeah the tired part is annoying. And that's nice it's not that bad. I threw up a lot with her, it was just the nausea."

"Oh I remember." She says amusement in her voice. I roll my eyes at that.

"Do you think people are going to talk?" She glances at me give me a pointed look before she looks back to the road.

"Yes, but who cares. You got this cute little princess that they will be jealous of." I smile glancing back to Maddison.

"I guess that's true."

We find seats on the bleachers close to the game. I take Maddison out of her car seat as the guys warm up on the field. I spot Alex within seconds, and he sees us. He starts jogging over a big grin on his face. I hear some whispering behind us, but I ignore them. "I'm so happy you two are here." He says.

"Me too." I say. His coach calls him over making him groan. He kisses my lips quick before kissing Maddison's head and jogging back onto the field.

"Bianca, is that you?" I turn to look at the girl behind me. Mini steps close as she turns to the girl too.

"Yeah, why?" I ask bouncing Maddison lightly. She fusses a little watching to see her daddy.

"It's been forever." She says her eyes going to my princess. "I guess I can see why." Her face is slightly discussed as she looks back to me.

"Say what you want about me, I really don't care. You say anything about my daughter and I won't hesitate to ruin you." I warn her. Her mouth slacks not ready for my response.

"What?"

"You heard her." Nini backs me up. I turn around to watch the players get set up on the field. Nini and I sit down sighing ready for the game to start.

"Is this seat taken?" I smile looking to Austin. He has Holly right behind him and I see the rest of them coming over.

"Nope, have a seat." He hugs me, careful of Maddison, before taking a seat. Ethan comes over with Nate also taking a seat ready to watch Alex and Chris play. Olivia comes to sit behind us with her boyfriend Cian, and Justin sits with them as well.

We all chat before seeing the other team set up before the referee brings the ball to the middle. As soon as the whistle blows we all start cheering.

I put noise canceling headphones on Maddison's ears not wanting to bother her as we were waiting. So, she just stays in my arms happy as Nini and I stand cheering for our men. We watch the two of them work together to make a goal gaining our team a point. As the game continues to go Chris and Alex keep getting scores, but the other team has been making some too.

With the last quarter coming to an end the teams are tied. Chris and Alex share a look and they play their famous move. Alex takes a pass to Chris and scores right towards the goal with Chris head butting it into the goal. Our side of the bleachers go wild as the referee blows the whistle ending the game.

Our big group all go onto the field leaving the car seat on the bench. Alex wraps sweat arms around me as he kissing my lips. He the lowers his head to kiss Maddison's head as she rests happily in my arms. I take the headphones off her making her fuss for a second. She looks up to Alex with a grin on her face. He picks her up and kisses all over her face making her laugh. He looks at her outfit and laughs looking to me.

"Very accurate." I nod my head smiling widely.

"I know. Congrats my love." I sing wrapping my arms around his sweaty waist, but I don't care. He laughs before I feel his lips on the top of my head.

"Okay you two, cut it out." I hear Austin. Olivia rolls her eyes at him before taking Maddison in her arms. Alex the grins before picking me up making me squeal. I wrap my legs around him and rest my forehead on his.

"Wow, why can't I have that?" Austin asks. I hear a smack before he groans in pain. "I was kidding."

"Nah, but for real you two are fucking goals." Nate says. Alex chuckles kissing my lips quick before letting me down gently.

"Take notes boys." Alex muses.

"Dude, really?" Chris raises an eyebrow at Alex. All Alex does is shrug in response.

"Congrats son. That was an amazing game." Justin claps Alex's back.

"I remember playing it." Austin sighs.

"Bro shut up." Olivia groans. "No one cares." She presses as she smiles at Maddison. He gasps I'm fake hurt a She dramatically rests a hand over his heart.

"Are you sure you want to marry him?" Justin asks.

"Dad! What the hell?" We all try to not laugh at him, but he makes it hard.

"I didn't say anything." He shrugs. Austin just stands there mouth dropped.

"Austin, go get the car seat and diaper bag." Holly tells him. He frowns before nodding his head, and walking back to the bleachers. Holly just smiles widely looking after him.

"Wow he actually listened." Ethan gasps pretending to be astonished. Holly just shakes her head at him.

"He's amazing. I can't wait to see what he will be like as a dad." She looks after him sighing.

"I don't want to see that yet." Alex says.

"I second that." Justin says. Holly looks to them before her eyes widen.

"I didn't mean now. I want to be married a few years first." She says with her cheeks tinting pink.

"Babe!" Austin calls coming back over.

"Yes?"

"I was thinking, can we get a puppy?" He asks.

"Just when I thought he was going to say something his age." Nate shakes his head.

"I can hear you."

"That was the point." Chris adds.

Chapter thirty seven: well shit

I watch Maddison sit on the floor looking at her aunt, who lays on her back on her play mat. It so weird to think that Cassidy is her aunt when she is younger than Maddison. Graduation was six months ago, and the looks on everyone's face made it worth it. Nini walks into the room groaning with her hand on her swollen belly.

"What's wrong?" I ask her trying to hide my amusement. She gives me a look making me look back to the babies.

"It's just the baby is heavy." I nod my head knowing the feeling all too well.

"Yeah, not pleasant. I remember that." I sigh at the memory. It makes me somewhat want another. Maddison is growing so fast, and I just want a little baby to hold.

"Oh no. I know that look." I look to Nini innocently.

"What look?"

"The 'I want a baby' look." I bite my lip looking back to Maddison as she crawls over to one of her toys. She has just started doing that, and now does it all the time. Nicole walks into the room, and picks Cassidy up.

"Awe my little girl." She coos. I smile at that before looking at Maddison put one of her toys in her mouth. She has been starting to teethe making her always bitting on those kind of toys.

"Nicole, Bianca already wants another one." Nini says rubbing her belly. Nicole raises an eyebrow at me. I feel my eyes widen from Nini's words.

"Really? I mean she is six months. I don't see why not starting for another." She shrugs.

"You were supposed to tell her no." Nini laughs. Nicole just grins before kissing Cassidy's head.

"I can't help it. I love babies." We all laugh at that knowing just how true it is.

"Alex and I are waiting though until she is at least one." I tell them. Nicole scoffs.

"Yeah right. You two want another."

"Alex does? Already?" Nicole laughs at my lack of knowing.

"Oh Bianca, have you met my son? As soon as that little princess was born he wanted another."

"I didn't know this." I say looking to Maddison before getting up, and picking her up. "I still think we are going to wait a little longer though."

"I get it."

"Yeah, school for him has been a little time consuming."

"Chris too. I'm happy they are at the same school." Nini adds. I nod agreeing.

"Yeah, they are like never around though." I frown.

"I have no clue what Chris plans when the baby is born." I sigh at that knowing just how she feels.

"You two didn't talk about it?" I ask. She bites her lip at the question.

"I mean for like two seconds. He said don't worry it will all be fine, and everything will work out." Nini shrugs.

"So, you aren't going to college?" I ask. She sighs rubbing her belly.

"Nope. He is against it, but I don't see a point to it." I laugh knowing Alex had the same response. Maddison starts crying making me pick her up, and bring her to the kitchen. I go to get a teething ring and give it to her. She takes it, and starts bitting it as I shut the freezer.

"Ugh girls I have to go. They need me at work." Nicole groans.

"I can watch Cassidy." I offer walking into the family room area. Nicole puts Cassidy in the swing as she yawns watching her mom.

"This way she can practice." Nini jokes making Nicole hold in a laugh. I shoot them both a look making Nicole clear her throat.

"Thank you honey." She blows me a kiss before leaving. I sigh looking to Nini, who frowns looking at her phone.

—

I narrow my eyes at him crossing my arms over my chest. He sits there looking guilty at his spot on the table. Nini drags Chris in by his ear, and makes him sit at the table next to Alex. They keep their head down as their eyes study the table.

"Care to explain?" I ask. Alex glances up to me.

"It wasn't me." He mumbles. I raise an eyebrow at him.

"Want to say that again?"

"I didn't do it." He says a little louder.

"Chris?" I look to him. He glances between Nini and I. He gulps swallow-ing hard.

"Okay, I ate them." He says.

"I knew it!" Nini and I shout loudly at the same time.

"How could you?" I ask. I really wanted to eat the cookies. We made brownie cookies today, and Nini and I have been eating them all day. They are so good, and Chris finished them.

"They were there so I ate them." He shrugs. Alex gives him a look letting him know he messed up.

"Are you kidding me right now?" Nini asks her eyes narrowed. "I've been craving them so bad, and you just eat them!" She tries to be quiet as Maddison sleeps in her room.

"I'm sorry baby, really." He tries, but Nini and I just shake our heads.

"Go get us stuff to make more." She orders him. He quickly jumps up to go get the stuff.

"Wait, let me come with you!" Alex rushes out as he stands up.

"Get me some Chinese food while you are out." I tell him. He nods his head, and the two of them hurry out. Nini sighs taking a seat in the chair.

"He better hurry."

"Oh trust me they will." She smiles nodding her head as she rubs her swollen belly. "Coming close to the due date." I grin. She gives me a nervous look.

"Yeah, were scared. At least I am. We just got our own place, and now everything is getting real."

"I know. At least on the bright side you are across the hall. If you need anything just knock or call us." I give her a reassuring hug.

"That's true. Everything is coming together."

"Exactly. Ugh they need to hurry I'm hungry." I pout. Nini chuckles at me, and we both quiet down hearing a cry. I get up and hurry to my daughter. She cries holding her pacifier in her hand.

I pick her up smiling down to her. I hear Nini scream in the kitchen making me hurry that way. She looks up to me worried.

"My water just broke." My eyes widen hearing her words.

"Well shit."_____________________Hope you liked it!

Sorry for the late update, I was on vacation with no WiFi

Let me know what you think Nini and Chris are having

Name ideas?

Chapter thrity eight: new baby

W e wait in the waiting room, with Maddison in my arms. Alex is sitting next to me with his leg bouncing up and down. His hand is on my knee as he holds on as I'm the only thing keeping him sane. Maddison is sleeping, after being confused for the past few hours. My mom offered to come get her, and said she is on her way. That was a little bit ago, so she should be here any minute.

"Why are you so nervous?"

"What if it's a boy? This can happen all over again." He whispers his words a little rushed. I shake my head at him.

"What if it's a girl, and they still get together?" I ask looking to him. He freezes looking to me before glancing down to our little princess.

"What? I mean if that's what they want, but this isn't funny right now Bee." I shrug a smile still on my lips.

"I thought it was." Alex rolls his eyes at me.

"Alex breathe, history doesn't have to repeat itself."

"It did for us." He points out.

"It didn't for your older siblings." I counter.

"Bianca." I turn to seem my mom. I grin at her as I stand up. She helps me get Maddison in the car seat without waking her up. My mom hugs me before looking to Alex.

"Don't ask." I laugh making him shoot me a glare.

"Oh Alex, relax. It's just a baby, and for all you know Maddison won't get along with them." He raises an eyebrow thinking about it making me roll my eyes.

"Thanks for watching her again mom."

"No problem honey." She says giving me another hug before picking the car seat up. "Keep my updated."

"Will do!" I call after her as she heads out. I look back to Alex, and sit on his lap. His arms automatically wrap around me holding me close to him.

"I want another one." He whispers in my ear. I sigh looking at him, so our eyes meet.

"Now?" I ask. He grins making me roll my eyes. "Alex, you just got in college and are busy with soccer." He frowns at me.

"I'll quit if you want. The school part I'll do, but not the sport part." He tries. "Chris talked to the coach. He can't play in games, and if he wants to practice with the team he can. This way be can still play what he loves."

"What's the point?" Alex shrugs.

"He wanted the two of us to still play."

"Well, that's stupid. You two aren't going to play in the future." I point out. "Oh did you see the new ideas I though of for the baby options for your shop?" I change the topic.

"No, where did you put them?" He asks smiling widely. I roll my eyes just as the doors open. Alex and I look to see Chris coming towards us. He looks tired as hell, but a grin is on his face. Alex and I get up and hurry to Chris.

"How did it go?" I ask at the same time Alex asks what the baby is. Chris rolls his eyes at Alex as he looks to me.

"It was long, but Nini did a beautiful job. Well she told me we aren't having another, but I know we will." He winks. I laugh knowing Chris will find a way.

"What did you two have?" I ask. He looks between the both us just grinning.

"Nope, you have to go see." Alex groans, and I just roll my eyes.

"Well, then why are we still here?" I ask. Chris chuckles before leading the way. Alex is uneasy next to me making me take his hand.

"Dude, why are you nervous?" Chris asks looking over his shoulder.

"Oh no reason." Alex says sounding as truthful as he can. Chris just laughs shaking his head.

"Yeah right."

"Okay, can we just see your baby?" I practically beg. Chris raises an eyebrow at me before looking back to where we are headed.

"Why are you begging?" Alex asks me amused.

"I love babies." I shrug. "How far is the room?" I whine. Chris stops and turns around to look at me.

"Are you really whining now? I don't need another baby right now. My newborn was just born." He points out.

"Oh Chris, just show us your baby." Alex laughs. Chris rolls his eyes at both of us.

"I'm sorry, it was just so stressful. I felt bad for Nini the whole time..." he trails off.

"Chris!" We almost shout at the same time. He stops and looks between the both of us.

"What?" He asks.

"Can we please see the baby?" Alex asks slightly annoyed.

"Please do you not realize how cute they are." I grin looking right into his eyes. I feel Alex give me a glance, but I ignore it.

"Fine." He sighs reaching to the door closest to us. He opens it and then grins at us. "Guys meet our little bundle of joy." He grins. We walk in eager as hell to see the baby. Nini is feeding the baby as she looks up, and grins at us.

"Did Chris tell you?" She asks. I shake my head walking closer.

"No, what is it?" Alex asks.

"A baby." Nini rolls her eyes jokingly. Alex sighs stepping to my side.

"Nini, what is the baby?" I ask trying to sneak a glance. She just laughs looking down the the little baby. I frown wanting another one.

"Alex, Bianca meet Joseph." Chris says behind us. I grins looking to him, and Alex just looks to him with wide eyes.

"Oh hell no." Alex states making me slap his arm. He looks to me frowning. "You hit me." He says cupping the part of the arm I smacked. I shrug at his pouting.

"Alex, what's wrong?" Nini asks.

"History is not going to repeat itself again." He declares. I roll my eyes looking right at Nini, who just looks amused.

Chapter thirty nine: seeing him

"**U**m are you there?" I blink at the voice realizing I zoned out.

"Physically, yes. Mentally that is debatable." I answer looking to Alex. He laughs rolling his eyes.

"Well, that's a start." I shake my head at him before looking in the back seat to Maddison's car seat. I have a little mirror that lets us see her face.

"Can we go get food now? I'm hungry and she's up." Alex laughs as he turns the car off.

"As you wish my Queen." I roll my eyes looking to him a stupid smile taking over my lips. He gets out of the car and hurries to my side. I roll my eyes as he opens the door before I can.

"I can do it you know." He nods his head.

"Oh I know, but I like to. Now let me get princess out." He says as he shuts my door. I follow him to her side and watch as he gets her out easily. She tries to grab at his face making me laugh.

"Not now princess." He tries, but she doesn't know any better.

"Bianca?"

"Alex?" We hear at the same time. We look at each other both tense before we turn around looking to see them. There stands AJ and one of his buddies from the old high school team.

"Wow, it is you two." AJ says stunned. Alex keeps Maddison close to him blocking her face as he holds her so her head is on his shoulder.

"Yeah, it's been a while." He says as I take a small step closer to Alex.

"See you're daughter hasn't changed you two." His buddy says.

"Nope. She's only made us stronger." Alex says dryly.

"Sure she has." He draws.

"What seems to be the problem over here?" Austin asks his arms crossed as he stands between us and the guys. AJ looks to him shrugging.

"Nothing, just a friendly conversation."

"Right. That's why they are so tense and protecting their daughter. If I were you I'd leave, or we can have a friendly chat." Austin smirks towards him. AJ gulps before him and the other one leave.

"Have your brother stand up for you every time right?" AJ calls over his shoulder.

"Oh I'm not standing up for him bitch. I just know what assholes you are AJ. I remember you and Tanner clearly, all the shit you pulled. If I see you again my buddies and I will teach you another lesson." Austin warns stepping towards him. I take Maddison from Alex and walk toward Holly, and Alex stands by Austin.

"You saw?" I ask. She frowns nodding her head.

"Yeah, we came out as Olivia had to be kept back. Claws were out." She laughs. I laugh too just imagining her going at the two of them.

"That would have been a sight." I agree.

"Come on, I'll show you where we are sitting." I nod my head before looking to Maddison who is yawning. I smile kissing her head before following Holly.

"How is Derrick?" I ask her.

"He fits in really well. I'm glad she found him, but I'm just going to warn you." She starts before stoping her steps.

"What?" I ask raising an eyebrow.

"He's a character." She laughs quietly.

"Oh great." I laugh with her. I've never really met the guy even though he went to my baby shower. He just has never been around when I have been over.

"Well, lets go." She grins. Maddison fusses making me move her in my arms. She plays with my earring as we walk to the table.

"Maddison!" Olivia cheers. I laugh as she seems to perk up. I look to Olivia amused that she is more excited to see my daughter.

"Well, hello to you too." I grin as she hugs me. I hug her back the best I can.

"Did those dicks leave? If not I'll gladly go out there at deal with them." I roll my eyes as she pulls back.

"Yes, it's all okay now." I look around her to see Derrick. He stands waiting for his turn to greet me.

"Where is my queen and my princess?" I hear Alex a little ways behind us. I bite my lip before turning around.

"Babe!" I call gaining his attention. He sees me and grins before coming to me. He wraps his arms around me pulling me close, but careful with Maddison. He kisses my head as his body relaxes.

"Bro really?" Austin groans.

"Come on man, they are just showing some love for each other." Derrick says amusement clear in his voice.

"But it's my brother, and someone that's basically my little sister."

"Oh Austin." Olivia sighs. Alex lets me go so we can all take our seats.

"Just for the record, if I ever see those mud monkeys again I won't hold back." Derrick says. We all look to him shocked as he sips on his drink.

"What?" Alex asks.

"Well, they must be dicks. Olivia wanted to rip with throats out and they seemed to have hit a nerve with all of you." He shrugs. Austin grins looking to Olivia.

"Marry him." Olivia chokes on her water as Austin then turns to Derrick. "We're going to tag team those bitches." He grins.

"Austin!" I gasp. "Maddison is here." He bites his lip looking to Maddison, who is sitting on my lap facing the table. She holds two forks in her hands and tries to bang them on the table.

"Sorry." Everyone just laughs, and even little Maddison laughs.

After ordering and chatting our food finally comes. I feel sick to my stomach as Austin's food is placed in front of him. The smell just hits my nose making my stomach churn. I quickly give Maddison to Alex before I'm up hurrying to the bathroom.

I lock myself in a stall as I wait to see if I have to empty my stomach. The feeling I'm my throat makes me spit into the toilet, but that's all I know. The door opens again and I can hear them lock the door.

"Bianca?" Olivia calls. I flush the toilet before opening the stall door. I walk to the sinks ignoring Olivia. I splash cold water in my face feeling a little better.

"Bianca, you okay?" She asks coming over to me. I nod my head before looking to her.

"Yeah. It's just whatever Austin was eating, like the smell of it just hit me the wrong way." I shrug. She frowns but nods her head anyway.

"Are you going to be able to sit out there and eat?"

"I don't know, but I can try. Maybe Alex will switch seats with me." I sigh.

"I'll just ask Derrick, this way all guys are on one side and you'll be a little farther from him." She smiles hugging me. I hug her back matching her smile.

"Thank you Olivia."

"No problem hun. We just won't bring much attention to this."

"Try to is more like it." I laugh. She pulls back rolling her eyes. We walk to the door and she unlocks it.

"Well, lets go try to then." She laughs as she leads me out. I laughed with her as we go towards the table. Alex gives me a look saying we'll talk later and I just give him a slight nod. Olivia tells Derrick to move, and he does without question. The smell is still there making my appetite go.

———————————————

Hope you guys liked it! Sorry it's been a while. Next update won't take as long I promise.

Thoughts?

Chapter forty: thank you

"Where are the mini M&Ms?" I ask pouting. Maddison is sleeping in the bedroom, and Alex is in the other room watching the game with Ethan and Nate. Chris and Nini were also going to come, but Joseph was giving them a hard time.

"I think we ran out!" Alex calls back. I groan walking into the room they are in pouting.

"Alex." I whine staying in my spot. He looks to me raising an eyebrow taking in my whole look.

"What?"

"I want them." I pout looking at him. He sighs standing up and walks over to me. He wraps his arms around me pulling me to him.

"Do you want me to go get you some?" He asks. I feel him looking down to me, and all I can do is nod my head yes. My head still rests on his chest, and he chuckles.

"Please."

"Okay, my Queen." He kisses my head before letting me go. I grin looking up at him, and he smiles before he moves around me and heads towards the door. "I'll be back guys." Alex calls over his shoulder.

"What's wrong with you?" Ethan asks looking at me wearily. I roll my eyes at him taking Alex's seat crossing my arms over my chest.

"Nothing. What's wrong with you?" He looks to Nate shocked before looking back to me.

"You're not pregnant are you?" Nate asks.

"No." I say through a yawn. They both look to each other before looking back to me.

"You need to take a test." Ethan says.

"What? No."

"Bee, go. Your boobs look a little bigger, you're tired and you're craving shit." Ethan says. I raise an eyebrow.

"Bro that came out wrong." Nate shakes his head.

"I realize that." He sighs looking down. "It's just noticeable." He shrugs. I look down seeing how they are kinda coming out of my bra. You can see it from the tank I wear under the flannel. I cover myself up feeling uncomfortable.

"I don't think so."

"When's the last time you had sex?" I gasp looking to Nate.

"Not for a while why does it matter?"

"Because you lose your sex drive." He rolls his eyes.

"How the fuck do you know all this?" I ask. Nate sighs looking to Ethan.

"Don't worry about it. Go take a test." He orders.

"I don't have any here." I tell him.

"E go get one I'll stay with her." Nate says handing keys over.

"I don't need to be watched." I roll my eyes.

—

Somehow Ethan got back before Alex, and he forced me to take the test. Maddison starts crying as he shuts the bathroom door on me.

"Let me help my daughter." I tel him as I try to open the door, but fail.

"Nate has her. Now take the damn test." Ethan orders. I groan as I walk to the toilet to pee on the stupid stick. After following the directions and washing my hands I wait.

"Queen?" I hear Alex call. I open the door knowing the time isn't close to when I have to check the test.

"Coming." I say with a smile. I walk in to see Nate sitting on the couch with no shirt and Maddison sleeping on his chest. "Um Nate?" I question. He looks between Alex and I before looking down to Maddison.

"I fed her, she pushed it away and it spilled on my tee shirt, so I took it off. I paced with her back and forth and she fell asleep." He explains.

"Oh." I say before looking to Alex. "Did you get it?" I ask eagerly. Alex chuckles nodding his head.

"Yes, Queen." He grins holding the bag up. I grin skipping to him and grabbing the bag. Ethan then stands up before walking towards the bathroom.

"I'm going to take a leak." He says, and I freeze for a second knowing why. But I walk into the kitchen with the bag wanting chocolate and whipped cream.

"Wait, you're going to leave her sleeping on me?" Nate asks trying to be quiet. I roll my eyes and Alex just laughs staying in the room with him.

"Hey, Bianca! Can you come here for a second?" Ethan calls making me groan. I stomp pass the two gaining amused looks as I walk towards the bathroom. As I get closer I feel nervousness hit me. My stomach flips not knowing what is going to be the answer. I get to the door and see Ethan standing there holding the test.

"You know I peed on that right?" I question lowly making him dropped it looking disgusted.

"That's gross, but Bee come look." He says pointing to it. I see the test and blink trying to see it clearly.

"Fuck." It leaves my lips without me realizing.

"What's wrong?" I hear Alex making me jump turning around to face him. I hear Ethan clear his throat before walking around me to the door.

"I'll leave you two alone for this." He says patting Alex's shoulder. Alex looks to me worried.

"Bianca, what's wrong?" I bite my lip as I grab the test and hand it to him. He looks at it for a little before looking up to me. "Was this Maddison's?" He asks unsure.

"No." I shake my head slightly tears stinging my eyes.

"I'm going to be a dad again?" He asks sounding in awe. I nod my head not being able to say anything. The news hitting me just like it's hitting him. He grins wrapping his arms around me and spinning me around.

"Did you just find out?" He asks in my ear. I nod my head as tears fall from my eyes. He holds me to him looking down at me. He wipes my tears before kissing my lips.

"We're going to have another." I smile looking into his eyes.

"Thank you." He grins kissing my lips again. I let out a small laugh as I wrap my arms around him.

"Why are you thanking me?"

"You gave me a beautiful daughter, and now we are having another baby." He lifts me up, and I wrap my legs around his waist.

"It takes two to tengo." I laugh as he walks us out of the bathroom.

"You two good?" Ethan asks.

"We're having another!" Alex cheers kissing me again before setting me down. We walk towards the living area, and see Maddison is awake. Alex picks her up and grins kissing her face.

"We're having another one like you." Alex tells her. I smile seeing all his excitement. I look to Nate and Ethan who smile too, and this time they won't miss any of it.

"Congratulations!" They cheer at the same time. Alex comes to me grinning, and hugs me with one arm as he holds Maddison in his other arm.

"Thanks guys. I can't wait for this." He looks to me and kisses my lips before kissing Maddison's head.

"Awe you guys are too cute." Nate says.

"Damn, Nate we need to find someone." Ethan says making me roll my eyes leaning into Alex and resting my head on his shoulder.

Chapter fourty one: wedding

"Stop fussing." I beg Maddison. She stops looking behind me and grins. I roll my eyes knowing she sees her father. I finish with the bow on her head, and smile at her little outfit. She is in a little pastel pink dress with a matching color bow. She is ready for her uncle and aunt's wedding. I wear a navy blue long flowing dress that is strapless with a sweetheart neckline.

"Are my girls ready?" I laugh looking to Alex as I stand. I put Maddison on the ground, and she runs to Alex. I smile at that walking over to Alex, who just picked Maddison up.

"Dada." She grins. He kisses her cheek grinning. She has started saying mama and dada last month, which made us both cry. Well, me more than Alex, but I blame the pregnancy hormones. I'm only three months, and we haven't told the family yet.

"We're ready. Is the rest of the wedding party ready?" He grins having his full attention on me.

"Yes, we just have to give Nate princess." He says as Maddison tries to reach for his hair. "No princess, not now."

"And this is why babies don't go to weddings." Nate groans as he walks into the room.

"Oh shut it, this is a special wedding." I tell him with a glare. He holds his hands up in mock surrender.

"Damn okay, calm the hormones." He says walking up and taking Maddison.

"Shh." Alex and I shush him at the same time.

"What?"

"They don't know." Alex tells him harshly.

"Don't know what?" Olivia asks coming into the room, followed by the bride to be.

"Shit." Nate whispers to himself before he quickly leaves the room. Alex and I look to each other before looking to them in front of us. Olivia stands there with her arms crossed over her chest.

"Alex." She draws as if she is talking to a little kid.

"What? Oh would you look at the time." He says before he tries to leave. Olivia grabs him by the arm giving him a glare.

"Alex please tell us, please don't make the bride upset." Holly pouts. Alex groans looking to me, and I just look to him nervous as hell.

"A little help here Bee?" Alex asks. I just wrap my arms around my waist afraid.

"Please Bianca." Holly pouts.

"Don't tell anyone, okay." I say.

"Well I might tell Austin, but that's it." She grins. I roll my eyes walking towards them. Olivia let's Alex go, and I wrap my arms around his waist.

"I'm pregnant." I smile. I glance up to see Alex grinning.

"Wait, really?" Holly gasps.

"I knew it!" Olivia claims. We all look to her making her roll her eyes. "That night a dinner a few months back. How far along?"

"Three months." I say resting a hand on the smallest baby bump I have hidden under my dress.

"Awe." Holly says happily. "We'll talk more about this after the wedding. Places people." She grins, and we listen ready to get this all started.

"Oh Holly?" I ask before heading off.

"Yeah?"

"I'm sorry you had to find out right now." I sigh looking down.

"Why?"

"It's your day." I tell her. She scoffs shaking her head.

"Oh Bianca it's an amazing gift." She hugs me tight making me smile.

—

I hold Maddison as I dance with her. Everyone is all happy and celebrating the marriage of Austin and Holly. I feel bad because only a handful of her family are here. I feel arms wrap around me making Maddison giggle as I lean into them.

"How are my girls?" Alex asks in my ear making chills go down my spine.

"Great." I say turning my head to kiss his cheek. He grins before meeting my lips with his. I smile when he pulls back and our eyes meet.

"What's that look for?" He asks.

"Nothing." I smile looking back to Maddison. She fusses in my arms and I put her down. She starts walking around before running off. I laugh following her, and Alex grabs my hand as we hurry after our daughter.

Austin squats down as Maddison runs into his arms. He grins saying her name making her laugh historically. He wraps his arms around her and picks her put. He looks to Holly saying something we can't hear.

"Looks like you found our princess." Alex says as we reach the newly weds. Austin grins looking to us.

"Yeah, congrats on number two." He grins wider. I hide my face in Alex's shoulder as they all chuckle.

"Thanks bro. Please don't tell anyone else. We want to tell them in a special way." Alex pleads with his brother.

"Will do, but just do it soon. Also don't have anymore until we have one." Austin says wrapping one arm around Holly. My head rests on his shoulder as I watch the two of them look at each other love in their eyes.

"We'll see." Alex says making me look up at him. Something shines in his eye, and I can't tell if he's joking or not.

Austin puts Maddison down just as his mom comes over with Cassidy walking as she holds Nicole's hands. I smile at that and seeing how happy Nicole seems. "This is crazy." She says as she reaches us.

"What?" Austin asks.

"My last baby is just walking, and my oldest just got married." She says glancing down at Cassidy. Then she looks to Alex and I. "And to top it off I'm a grandma." She laughs.

"Is that a bad thing though?" Austin asks. Nicole rolls her eyes shooting him a look. I look down to see Cassidy and Maddison tying to walk away.

"I would have said that idiot." She rolls her eyes.

"Maddison." I call ignoring them as I look to my daughter with a raised eyebrow.

"Mama." She smiles.

"Come here, my love." I tell her, and she runs this way. I squat down opening my arms for her, and she runs right into me. I laugh picking her up and kissing all over her face. She laughs grinning as she tries to move away.

"Awe." I hear Austin's grandma say. I look up to her and smile as Alex wraps his arms around me. I see Nicole is walking Cassidy towards Justin, and Austin and Holly are making their rounds to other family members.

"Hi grandma." Alex says letting me go to hug her.

"It's been a while boy." She says. This is his father's mother. She is the one that's been most supportive to his family. His other grandparents had a falling out with Nicole.

"I'm sorry, but I've been busy." He says letting her go. She looks to Maddison and me grinning.

"I figured. How are you all doing?" She asks.

"Great." I grin stepping closer. "Want to hold little Maddison?" She eagerly nods her head making me laugh as I hand her over. She hasn't seen Maddison since she has been born.

"Awe she's so precious." She says happily. "You two need to come over more. I'm finally moved back." She tells Alex giving him a stern look.

"Of course we will." He grins wrapping his arms around me.

Chapter fourty two: its a....!

"So, are you two going to find the gender out before?" Nini asks as she bounces Joseph on her lap. I finish dressing Maddison before putting her on the floor. She walks to her toys before dropping to the ground and playing.

"Yes, we both are eager to find out. I just don't know what this means for school now." I've been keeping up with my classes when Alex is watching her, or even when I can during the day when she is occupied.

"You'll figure it out. Just get through this semester first, and then talk about it." Nini smiles. I nod my head agreeing before I get up and head to the kitchen. I walk about out with a piece of a cookie brownie. Nini gives me a look as I shove the piece in my mouth.

"What?" I ask with a mouth full of food.

"Oh nothing." She rolls her eyes. "Oh! Can I throw your gender reveal party?" She asks eagerly.

"Why?" I raise an eyebrow at her.

"I' always wanted to do one for you, and it'll be so much fun." She grins. I sigh looking to Maddison as Nini puts Joseph down. He crawls over to

Maddison wanting to play with her. I look back to Nini with a smile on my face.

"Okay." Then something dawns on me making me frown.

"What's wrong?" Nini asks concern clear in her voice.

"Where are we going to have this little one sleep? You know as well as I do that this place only has one extra room, and that's Maddison's room."

"Oh I didn't think of that. You should bring that up to Alex, but at least for a little the baby can sleep in your room with you." She tries to assure me.

"That's true. Damn shit just got more stressful." I sigh leaning back in the couch. Nini laughs and I can see her shake her head out of the corner of my eye. I just watch the kids ignoring her completely. The door opens gaining our attention. Maddison stands up grinning.

"I'm back!" Alex announces. Maddison squeals before running to him.

"Dada!" He grins squatting down as she nears him. As soon as she reaches him he scoops her up in his arms making her squeal again. He kisses her face as he stands up straight with her.

Joseph crawls towards Chris making a grin break across his lips. "Awe who is daddy's little boy?" Chris asks in his baby voice as he picks Joseph up. I focus back to Alex and our princess as he comes towards me.

"How is my pregnant queen doing?" He asks sitting down next to me. He rubs one hand over the baby bump and kisses my cheek. I smile as Maddison laughs.

"I'm doing fine, the baby is doing fine." I sigh. He looks into my eyes reading them.

"What's wrong?" He asks, but it sounds like more of a demand. I roll my eyes trying to just ignore him.

"You two staying for dinner?" I ask looking to Nini and Chris. They look to each other then to Alex before Nini looks to Chris.

"Not tonight, sorry."

"It's fine." I shrug.

"Well, I guess we should get going." Nini says standing up and grabbing the diaper bag.

"Okay, bye guys." I wave from my seat because Alex won't let me up. Chris ushers them out and once they are gone I'm forced to look at Alex.

"Bianca, what's going on?" Alex asks, but it sounds more like a demand. I sigh shaking my head and putting a smile on my lips.

"Nothing is wrong, love. It's just our household is growing and we don't have enough rooms." He puts Maddison down before cupping my face in his hands.

"We'll just have to start looking, but we have some time. So, don't stress over it." He kisses my lips quick before he reaches down to Maddison and goes to play with her and her toys.

—

I hold the puppy in my arms. He squirms excitedly as he licks my ear. I laugh before putting the little guy down. He chases after Maddison making her squeal. Joseph runs after her with Chris' help. Cassidy sits eating fruit with her mom.

Austin grins at his puppy playing with the kids. It's a little soft coated wheaten terrier, and he is the cutest thing. His name is Teddy, and he is four months old.

"Awe babe, look at our little boy playing with the kids." He wraps his arms around Holly making her laugh.

"When can we find out?" Nate whines.

"Oh grow up." My Mom says coming over. "You sound like your father." She adds shooting him a look.

"Is that a good thing?" He asks. She gives him a look before looking over her should at his father. He is trying to prove he can to the water bottle flip thing. She looks back at him.

"That's for you to decide." She shrugs making Alex and I try to hold on a laugh.

"I guess it's time to find out." Nini says eagerly. I grin looking to excited to finally find out. "Let me just go set up, so you two go stand by the fence." She orders us.

"Come on my Queen." Alex grins holding his hand out for me. I take it before we head to where Nini told us. Everyone starts to gather around us waiting eagerly. Maddison comes over happily before Alex picks her up.

"What do you think princess? It is a Prince or a princess?" Alex asks her. She seems to think about it before frowning.

"No no." She pouts. I smile kissing her cheek.

"Want me to take her?" I look over to see Holly offered.

"Yeah, can you?" She nods her head and takes Maddison from Alex. Nini comes out with a soccer ball in her hands. Instead of the black and white it's the black switches with pink and blue.

"Alright soccer star, kick it and either pink or blue will come out." Nini explains giving it to Alex. He grins as everyone takes steps back to give us room. He looks to me kissing my lips before he puts the ball on the ground.

He kick the ball sending blue to explode from it . Everyone cheers with joy as I cry as I look to Alex wrapping my arms around him. His arms wrap around me as his lips meet mine.

"We're having a little prince." He grins. I grins back looking at him through my tears kissing him again.

"Congratulations you two!" I hear Austin cheer. Everyone adds in their own congratulations as they all come towards us. I let go of Alex to go hug everyone else. Our family is growing with our daughter and now son on the way.

Chapter fourty three: Epilogue

I groan burying my face into Alex more ignoring the noise. Alex chuckles holding me close to him. "Mommy Daddy wake up!" Maddison screams excitedly.

"It's Christmas!" Jared adds. I open my eyes looking right up at Alex.

"I want more sleep." Alex just shakes his head trying not to laugh. I playfully hit him not wanting to hear him laugh.

"Time to get up, we have a long day ahead of us." He says sitting up. He then freezes wrapping the sheets more around me, and his lower half.

"Oh sh-"

"Kids go wait in your rooms, and mommy and daddy will be there in a second." Alex says cutting me off.

"What about Parky?" Jared whines.

"You are not waking your cousin." Alex says sternly. Austin and Holly spent the night here with their son and dog. They had their son a little over a year ago, and since then Alex has wondered about a third. So, I hope he likes his Christmas gift.

"But daddy." Jared whines pouting his lips.

"No buts mister. If we hear that you woke him you will have to give away all the toys Santa gave you." Alex says sternly. Their eyes widen before they run out and hurry to their room. I just shake my head looking to Alex.

"Babe," I sigh gaining his attention.

"What?" He asks innocently as he gets out of bed. I watch him walk into our closet only to come back out with sweatpants which hang low on his hips. I bite my lip as I take in his torso ending on his tattoo before his chuckles make me look away.

"Why did you say that to them?" I say after clearing my throat. I look back to him only to see him shrug.

"I knew it would make them listen. Now, come on and hurry up. Austin is not one to wait." I laugh nodding my head. He is very true with that. I go to get dressed ignoring the nausea as I find black sweatpants and one of Alex's blue sweatshirts. He throws on a tee shirt before grinning at me.

"What?"

"I love when you wear my clothes." He says wrapping his arms around me. I smile and press a small kiss to his lips. There is a knock on our door making Alex groan.

"Will you two get a move on. The kids are about to run down the stairs already." Austin says. We open the door smiling at him to see him happy as ever. Austin is holding his little boy in his arms looking just as eager as him.

"You mean you?" Alex asks. Austin rolls his eyes, but I see Holly nodding her head behind him. I laugh before looking to the kids who are literally jumping up and down.

"Mommy go?" Maddison asks.

"Yes princess." I grin. The kids cheer, as does Austin and they all run , well scoot, downstairs. Teddy follows after them barking happily. Alex hurries after them while Holly and I share a look.

"He still doesn't know?" She asks. I smile shaking my head. I had to tell someone and she ran into me when I was getting the tests. "I can't wait to see his reaction."

"I know it'll be great." I grin.

"Queen come on!" Alex calls. We hurry down the stairs and into the family room to see the kids already ripping into their gifts. I smile watching them before closing my eyes feeling nauseous again.

"What's wrong?" Alex asks in a whisper as his arm wraps around me. I open my eyes looking to him before smiling.

"Can I give you your gift now?" I ask bitting my lip. He raises an eyebrow before looking around the room. "Not that kind of gift." I playfully swat him.

"Okay okay." He laughs. "And yes please my love." He grins kissing my forehead. I smile standing up looking to the kids. Wrapping paper ripped up all around them as the squeal over their gifts.

I get the box for Alex. I sit back next to him giving Holly a look. I hand it to him smiling, and he takes it grinning. "You know I don't need anything though Queen." He starts opening it and I feel nervous. I look to Holly, and both her and Austin watch us.

I look towards the kids to see our four year old and three year old helping Parker Open his gift. I smile at them before looking to Alex. He looks confused as he reads the two tee shirts. I bite my lip as he looks up to me.

"Do you not like it?" The nervousness makes my stomach churn.

"I'm confused. This one makes sense for princess, but for our prince I'm not sure." He says holding up both of them. They are both black, but one says 'world's best big sister' and the other says 'world's best big brother'. I hear Holly try to keep Austin quiet for us, but it's hard.

"Really?" I ask. He nods his head looking down to the shirts before his head snaps up to me.

"Wait! Are you saying what I think your saying?" He asks eagerly. His eyes shine with excitement making me smile widely. My eyes sting from the tears, but I ignore it. I nod my head making Alex tackle me in a hug.

"Congratulations!" Austin and Holly cheer at the same time. We look to them grinning before the kids. They look to us happily each lifting a toy they want open.

"Well let's open these toys!" Austin cheers getting up to help them.

"Thank you." Alex says kissing my cheek. I smile kissing his lips quick.

"I don't know how the kids will take it though." I say glancing to them. He chuckles hugging me close.

"They will be fine. But, come on there are more presents for everyone."

"Okay." I sigh getting up. Alex then stops and looks to me pouting. "What?"

"Why am I never there with you when you take the test and find out?" I roll my eyes poking his nose playfully.

"One: I don't want to get your hopes up, and two: I like surprising you." With that I get up leaving him there. I sit on the floor pulling Jared on my lap.

"Can I be there for the next one?" He asks. My jaw drops as I look to him.

"Next one?" I choke. "What if I want to be done after this one?" He frowns before smirking with a glint in his eyes.

"We'll see." I roll my eyes kissing Jared's head. I never thought Alex wanted that many kids. I'm good for now with the two we have and third on the way, but I guess we will have to see what the future holds. After a few more gifts Alex gives me one, a small little box. My mouth drops as I open it and he takes Jared off my lap.

"Will you marry me Bianca?" He asks, and the room goes quiet. The kids all look to us as does Austin and Holly.

"Yes!" I nearly shout wrapping my arms around him.

"Wow, first a baby and now a ring." Austin says.

"This was a very good Christmas, and it's only the morning." Holly grins. I laugh staying in Alex's arms. I will finally get to marry my best friend after three kids, and I wouldn't have it any other way.___________________